Petteril's Folly
Lord Petteril Mysteries, Book 6
Mary Lancaster

Petteril's Folly

DEDICATION

To Pam Labbe and Diane Gillis who have proved invaluable to Lord Petteril.

Chapter One

"*Is it time?*"

April, Viscountess Petteril, placed both hands on the balustrade and breathed in the warm, sea air of Portugal. This gracious house with its arches and courtyards had been home for the last few days, as had the view beyond the balcony to the gentle cliffs and the crashing ocean, the circling sea gulls above, and the whitewashed village to her left, with its pretty harbour and fishing boats.

If paradise existed, she thought, it would be here, with this rare man lounging at her side. She closed her eyes, smiling, and lifted her face to the lowering, evening sun, listening to the sea and the birds, and the soft sigh of her companion.

"Is it time?" asked her husband, whom she could now call Petteril, or even Piers, rather than *my lord*. Or *mister*.

He had been watching her, she knew, but when she opened her eyes, he was gazing out to sea—this strange, quixotic gentleman, kind and unworldly, yet alarmingly sharp. She wasn't sure how he had come to mean more to her than the air she breathed, but he did.

She shouldn't have married him, of course. He had offered from mere honour, an honour that was certainly not due to a girl like her, a thief from the back streets of St. Giles. Her own reasons for accepting were much more complicated. She had taken a risk, and here in Portugal, it had been wonderful.

They had been married at a drumhead wedding in Spain, performed by a regimental chaplain and witnessed by Petteril's cousin, Major Bertie Withan, and several of his amiable fellow officers. That in itself had been an adventure. And then they had spent the next four weeks on a wedding journey, following their noses while avoiding signs of war, exploring where they liked and staying wherever they could, whether at a basic inn, or a beautiful, borrowed house like this one.

They had admired castles and scenery, explored medieval towns and walked on smooth, sandy beaches. They had laughed and bantered with each other and with indulgent local people encountered en route, behaving, probably, like children. She had never seen him so devoted to relaxation and it was intoxicating.

Still, she had known it couldn't last. Sooner or later, one had to face reality. And she had sensed his restlessness in the last few days. In truth she had felt it herself. She had chosen her path for her own reasons, and she needed to deal with the consequences before they loomed any larger.

"Yes," she said sadly. "It is time. We can be back in Lisbon tomorrow."

They turned and walked into the house together.

The borrowed servant brought them tea and port wine, bowed, and departed. April drank a glass of port with him, because she liked the taste and the companionship. By the time it was gone, night had fallen. She rose and he doused the lights, then followed her into the beautiful, arched courtyard.

They took a candle each from the foot of the stairs and climbed together.

He opened the first door for her, and she brushed past him into the bedchamber beyond.

"Good night, April."

"Good night, my lord." She closed the door behind her and remained leaning against it, listening to his footfalls cross the landing away from her.

TWO WEEKS LATER, THE Petteril crested traveling coach disgorged them at the front steps of the viscount's chief seat, Haybury Court.

April, her nerves wound tight as a drum in her fashionable new morning gown, purchased in Lisbon, felt stiff and scared, almost like the first time she had come here, facing the suspicion and the contempt of the servants. Then, of course, she had been one of them, to all intents and purposes. Now she was their mistress. Which certainly gave her the power to punish any insolence, but she had been below stairs in enough houses to recognize that servants had their own ways of venting resentment.

The trouble was, she had grown fond of them, even prickly Mrs. Hicks, the housekeeper. And what would Mr. Stewart—whom she must remember to call simply Stewart now—his lordship's valet, think? He would believe—they would *all* believe—that she had inveigled the viscount into marriage, that such had always been her intent.

Petteril took her hand and placed it on his arm. He squeezed her fingers and she raised her head, refusing to let him down.

Just like the first time, the servants spilled out of the house and around from the stables to welcome them. At the head of the hastily formed line stood plump Mrs. Hicks and a thin upright man, almost totally bald. He must be the new butler. She did not so much as glance at the other servants yet, though she knew they were all there.

"Mrs. Hicks, how are you?" Petteril greeted the housekeeper.

"All the better to see you home, my lord, and to be able to welcome your lady." She curtsied twice, beaming at each of them. Bizarrely, if she recognized April, she gave no sign of it. "And I'm sure you remember Barlow."

Barlow was the butler he had engaged just before he left for Portugal.

"Of course, I do," Petteril lied. He never remembered anyone's face. He only knew Mrs. Hicks because she couldn't have been anyone else.

Barlow bowed reverentially and welcomed his lord and lady home. He then introduced each member of staff they passed on their way into the house, presumably to April. As if nobody had told him who she was.

She had been prepared to face resentment, contempt, dislike, but she had not envisioned being introduced to her old colleagues as a stranger. So she played the role of the viscountess she had been practising, a gracious smile on her lips, sparing each maid and manservant a nod of acknowledgement. Their expressions, so far as she could tell in her lightning glimpses, were avid, curious, but very respectful.

Had she agonized over this meeting for nothing? Did they really not mind about her elevation above them?

"I am happy to report," Barlow said as they entered the house, "that her ladyship's rooms have been refurbished and decorated as you requested."

"I expect your ladyship would like to see them first," Mrs. Hicks said.

"Perhaps tea in the drawing room, my lord?" Barlow suggested.

"Tea in the library, I think," Petteril said. "We'll just nip up and see what they've done to her ladyship's apartments."

As part of her duties in the spring, April had planned the refurbishment of many of the neglected rooms at Haybury Court, but the viscountess's accommodation had never been high on Petteril's agenda, and she had had nothing to do with any changes. Lord Petteril himself must have ordered it from Portugal. Curiosity began to overcome her rigid fear.

No one would have known it from Petteril's expression, but she knew from the very fact that he veiled it, that he wanted her to like the rooms. And they were so large and grand they made her previous chamber here—the one she had been so proud of, the first ever place she could call her own—seem almost like a hovel.

Her new apartments had been so well aired, that no smell of paint or varnish lingered. Instead, they smelled fresh, with several vases of flowers scattered throughout. Her sitting room was delightful, sunny yellow and cream, the carpets gold with a hint of red. An elegant little desk, several upholstered chairs, some small tables and a bookcase were tastefully placed. From the south facing windows, one of which was partly open, she could look down on the gardens and smell the lingering scent of late summer flowers.

The bedchamber, containing a mighty four-poster bed with ornate gold and black brocade curtains, continued the colour scheme. It was furnished with a large wardrobe, and a fine, mirrored dressing table, bedside tables and another bookcase. Off it was another, smaller chamber containing a washstand with fine porcelain bowl and jug, two chests of drawers and a large bath tub.

April was speechless.

Petteril said, "They've done well. Do you like it, my dear?"

The "my dear" still jolted her—fortunately, since at least it brought back her power of speech.

"It's beautiful," she whispered, and cleared her throat. "So delightful and comfortable."

"You must choose your own pictures for the walls, of course, and you will have your own books and knick-knacks to make it just as you like."

"It *is* just as I like," she said, walking back into the sitting room and twirling around, admiring the high, panelled ceiling and ornate cornice. *So much space... I can breathe*!

And suddenly it wasn't frightening at all. This was her private space, her supremely elegant bolt hole. She smiled at Petteril and his face relaxed.

"Let's go and have tea," she said gaily.

"Very well." He turned to go and addressed Mrs. Hicks. "Tell Stewart I shall want him in an hour, if you please. That should give him plenty of time to unpack."

"Ah." For the first time, Mrs. Hicks looked anxious. "Stewart. There's a slight problem with Stewart, my lord."

"There is? Is he unwell?"

"Oh no, sir. He's...um...he's been taken up by the magistrate."

Lord Petteril blinked. "*Stewart* has? What did he do? Get bosky and thump someone? Though to be fair, I have never seen him in his cups."

"No, my lord," Mrs. Hicks said, tight-lipped with disapproval at such levity. "He is accused of stealing."

Servants were always the first to be accused when something went missing, and so April was about to say, quite indignant on Mr. Stewart's behalf.

But before she could speak, Lord Petteril said briskly, "Nonsense. I don't believe it for an instant. I shall go directly to Mr. Lindon and bring him home."

"After tea, my lord," Mrs. Hicks reminded him.

Petteril opened his mouth, glanced at April and closed it again. "After tea," he agreed, ushering both women in front of him. "What is Stewart meant to have stolen?"

"Money, so they say. From the Red Lion, where he was with an old friend visiting in the area."

"Now I *know* it's rubbish. When did this happen?"

"Just yesterday. You could have knocked me down with a feather, I was so shocked. And of course it was the last thing we needed, what with you and Lady Petteril expected any moment."

If it hadn't been for the sudden anxiety over Stewart, April would have welcomed her return to the Haybury Court library, where, in the past, she had spent precious time alone with Lord Petteril. More time than she should have, probably. Then, she had often knelt on the floor at his feet to discuss things. Now, she sat in the chair opposite, and the tea tray was placed on a small table in front of her.

"Thank you," Petteril said to Patrick the first footman who brought it. "Her ladyship will pour."

It was an art April had been practising. Her own inclination was simply to slosh the stuff into vessels and ladle in a load of sugar and milk. Until she went to Portugal, she had never drunk out of fine porcelain teacups. Now, however, she poured the tea with elegance, and his lordship rose gravely to take the cup and saucer from her. His lips quirked in acknowledgement of her grace.

Primly, she poured her own.

As soon as the door closed behind Patrick, she said, "Stewart never stole anything. It's not in his nature."

"There must be some misunderstanding," Petteril agreed. "I'll sort it out with Lindon."

"I don't suppose he likes valets very much." In the spring when they had come here, Lindon had discovered that his wife was having an illicit liaison with a valet, an affair that had led to a great deal of tragedy.

"No," sighed Petteril. "But it's hardly fair that Stewart should suffer for it." He hesitated, then said, "Do you want to come with me?"

Before, she would have jumped at the chance. Now, she had no idea how—or even if —Mrs. Lindon would receive her since she was a jumped up maid-assistant raised to be a viscountess who outranked her so unfairly. It would have to be faced, of course, but perhaps not just yet...

She shook her head. "I'll stay here and organize my things. They're taking it very well, aren't they? Better than I had ever hoped."

"So far. Just remember, keep your temper with any insolence and report it to me."

"You won't dismiss anyone?" she said anxiously.

"Not for a first offense," he replied, looking vague. His mind, she suspected, was already on extracting Stewart from the clutches of the magistrate. Which was just as it should be, for Stewart was a good man and loyal in his quiet yet somehow impressive way.

They did not linger over tea but separated at the library door. April went up to her own apartments, preparing to be awed all over again. It seemed incredible that this too she would get used to, like being a girl, and then a pretend lady, and then the real Lady Petteril.

However, as soon as she entered, she heard movement from the bedchamber, and found Mrs. Hicks there, unpacking her trunks (she had two trunks to herself, now) and placing everything in neat piles upon the bed.

"My lady. I hear you don't yet have a maid, so I thought I'd put these things away for you, rather than let Mavis loose about them. She's excellent with a duster, but—"

"Oh, just this once I'd like to do it myself," April said. "Then I can decide at the same time exactly where I want everything."

"Very good, my lady." Mrs. Hicks managed to look both relieved and aggrieved. "Is there a time you would like to go over menus, inventories and so on?"

"Tomorrow morning, I think. Thank you, Mrs. Hicks."

It felt very odd dismissing the housekeeper who had been in charge of her only weeks ago, but the woman left with a respectful little bow.

It was odd, but still April saw no recognition in her eyes. Did Mrs. Hicks *really* not recognize her? What exactly had Petteril said about her?

Catching sight of herself in the glass, April saw the same slightly snub nose she was used to, the same wide mouth and over-curious blue eyes. But her skin was rosier and smoother, her pallor vanished with nourishment and the Iberian sun. And her hair was very different. No longer short, straggly, and hidden under a mob cap, it had been fashionably cut in Lisbon and now framed her face elegantly, held in place by Spanish combs. Her neck, chest and shoulders had never been so vis-

ible in a cut-down maid's dress. And no one knew better than April that
people tended to see only what they expected.

Which probably meant Petteril had merely written to say he was
bringing home his bride, without mentioning her name. Indeed, why
would he to the servants? And April, in all her new finery, new accent,
and ladylike grace, was apparently unrecognizable to people she had
worked alongside only a few months ago.

This pleased her in some ways. In others, it made her sad. She had
wanted to be honest in her life with Lord Petteril, however that life
worked out, yet how undignified to wave her hands in front of the servants and announce gleefully that she was April. Still, she missed being
April. She missed being Ape, even if she didn't miss the daily struggle
for survival.

To distract herself, she set about being Lady Petteril, putting away
her gowns and nightgowns, chemises and petticoats, stockings and
shoes, shawls, pelisses, cloaks, hats, and riding habit. She put her per-
fume and her hairbrushes on the dressing table, along with a box Petteril had given her to put her jewels in. Jewels! That they were hers still
stunned her.

She took her soaps, oils and toothpowder into the dressing room.

After that, she set about placing her books, a few borrowed from
Lord Petteril, a few bought in Portugal, and the few trinkets she had
found in market stalls and pretty shops in Lisbon.

If she rang the bell, one of the footmen would come and take
her trunks away. She could order water for a bath and change into an
evening gown for dinner. Ladies, she had discovered, spent an inordi-
nate amount of time changing their dress for each trivial event. Morning dresses, walking dresses, riding habits, evening gowns... She had ex-
amples of each now, although ladies of the ton might sneer at the quan-
tity.

Well, the ladies of the ton would definitely sneer at *her*.

Who cares? I can sneer back rather better.

The sitting room desk was already furnished with beautiful paper, ink and pens. Remembering, she fetched the bag she had carried herself, and took out the notebook she had carried to Portugal and filled with notes in their search for Petteril's cousin Bertie.

She would need another now. Putting it away in one of the drawers, she decided to fetch a fresh one from the library, along with a few more books. Now that her reading had improved so much, she wanted to devour books on history and science and travel to other exotic countries. And novels. She was addicted to those, though some were so far-fetched they made her laugh.

She was in the library, making two neat little piles of books on the table, when Mavis stuck her head around the door, looking both anxious and avid.

"Lady Petteril, Lady Petteril has called!"

Chapter Two

At Lindon Grange, home of generations of Lindons since time immemorial, Piers was shown immediately into the magistrate's study.

Here, Lindon leapt to his feet, beaming. "My lord! Welcome home."

"Thank you." Piers allowed his hand to be heartily wrung.

"And congratulations are in order, we hear! Wish you very happy, Petteril, very happy indeed. Be assured my wife will call on Lady Petteril as soon as she is settled in."

Piers, already uneasy over the lack of reaction by his own staff to his bride, regarded him quite closely but could see no signs of insincerity. Of course, both Mr. and Mrs. Lindon regarded him as something of a hero for the way he dealt with their son's death, keeping the awful truth from public gossip.

"Thank you, you're very good." Piers said.

"Have a glass of wine?"

"Thank you."

"Sit down, my lord," Lindon said, almost in his old, jovial manner. Only when one looked closely were the lines of grief visible in his too-thin face, the signs of a man old before his time, not broken, exactly, but certainly bent with the weight of tragedy. "I suppose you've come about this sad business with your man."

"Stewart, yes. Mrs. Hicks says he has been accused of theft which I find astonishing. How did this all come about?"

Lindon sighed, presented him with a glass of wine from the decanter at his side, and sat down opposite him, raising his glass. "Jug-bitten, I expect. Not one to frequent taprooms by all accounts, but he was certainly in the Red Lion, night before last. One of the guests, Sir Darius Camden, had his purse vanish."

"In the taproom?"

"No, from his bedchamber. He and his sister are staying at the inn. He had a brandy in the taproom, and when he woke up the next morning, he found his purse had vanished from the table in his room where he put it."

"Where he put it on his return from the taproom?" Piers asked.

"No, no, he didn't take it to the taproom."

Or doesn't remember taking it, Piers thought cynically. "So how on earth does anyone come to blame Stewart for the disappearance?" He was careful not to call it theft, since he very much doubted it was.

"That's the rub," Lindon said ruefully. "Stewart was drinking with his friend, one Neil Murray, when Sir Darius entered the taproom. During his visit, Stewart accompanied Murray —who is also staying at the inn—to his room. A few minutes later, Stewart came downstairs and left the inn, presumably with Sir Darius's purse."

Piers pounced. "Presumably? Then you did not find the purse on Stewart's person?"

"No, which is the only reason I haven't charged him yet."

"You might as justly charge his friend, or anyone else for that matter. If Sir Darius didn't notice it had gone until the following morning, it could have been taken—if taken it was—long after Stewart had left the inn."

"As I say, he is not yet charged, but it does look bad for him."

Piers rubbed his chin. "Am I missing something? Why does it look worse for Stewart than anyone else who was at the inn during that night and early morning?"

"Because his friend Murray, says Stewart merely bundled him into his room and left, spending mere seconds there. And yet it was at least ten minutes, according to Barnes—the innkeeper, if you recall—before Stewart came down again. Time enough to pick a lock and steal the purse."

Piers regarded him until his eyes dropped. "Sir, I think you know that is insufficient evidence," he said quietly. "Especially against a man of good character. I am prepared to vouch for his honesty. Release him into my charge and I will help you find out who really stole this purse."

Lindon hesitated, pulling at his lip. "If it were anyone but you asking... Barnes believes his guests, you know."

"But not his other customers?"

"He doesn't know Stewart," Lindon protested. "The man tends to keep himself to himself; he's hardly ever at the Red Lion. Maybe no reason to doubt him, but no reason to trust him either."

"Then I hope you trust *me* enough to grant my request."

"Of course," Lindon said. "But you're not to send him out of my jurisdiction."

"As if I would. It's in his interests and mine to clear his reputation. Will you have him brought to me now?"

Lindon got up and rang the bell.

Five minutes later, two constables marched Stewart in between them.

The man was pale but otherwise looked unharmed. His normally immaculate clothing was rumpled, since he had slept in it, if he had slept at all, and his hair looked as if it needed a comb, but he still retained his proud bearing.

Until, catching sight of his master, he suddenly halted, taking his escort by surprise.

His eyes widened and his white face suffused with colour. "My lord! I'm sorry I could not be in attendance for your return."

"So am I," Petteril said, rising to his feet. "Mr. Lindon and I are agreed that the evidence against you is too flimsy to charge you, so you will return to Haybury Court with me." He bowed to Lindon. "Your servant, sir. My thanks for the wine and my valet. Bustle about, Stewart..."

In the carriage, Stewart sat opposite Piers on the back-facing seat. "I'm sorry you've come home to this."

"So am I. What the devil happened?"

Stewart gazed out of the window, gathering his thoughts, Piers guessed. "I received a note from the Red Lion, from an old acquaintance from Scotland. He found himself in the area and discovered I worked for you at Haybury Court. So he invited me to meet him at the inn. My duties are hardly arduous when you are absent, so I went."

Piers nodded. It was hardly unreasonable.

"We had a pleasant enough evening, recalling mutual friends and learning each other's news."

"Did you notice this fellow Camden—Sir Darius—in the taproom?" Piers interrupted.

"Only vaguely."

"Why did you go upstairs?"

Stewart sighed. "Murray was a trifle disguised. He must have been drinking all day. I could see that if I didn't take him up to his room someone else would have to."

"Was he unsteady on his feet?" Piers asked.

"A bit, though not as bad as I'd thought. I didn't need to hold him up, but he clutched the banister all the way upstairs."

"How long were you in his room?"

"Just a minute or two. He took off his boots and flopped on the bed, I pulled a blanket over him and left."

"Barnes said you were ten minutes."

Stewart brought his gaze back from the window at last. "I can't account for that."

"I think you can," Piers said steadily.

Stewart's lips twitched into an unhappy smile. "Not very convincingly. When I left Murray, I sat down on the top step and thought about the different ways our lives had gone since leaving home. Perhaps I was boskier than I thought. But I certainly didn't go into any other room. I couldn't even tell you which room belonged to this Sir Darius."

"Did you see anyone else while you were up there? Going in or out of the rooms? Guests? Servants? Staff?"

Stewart shook his head. "That's why they picked on me."

"Dashed unfair when Camden didn't even notice it was missing until the next day," Piers said.

Stewart met his gaze fully at last. "Then you believe me that I did not steal the purse?"

"Yes," Piers said. "But it's quite possible they will never find out who did. If anyone did. And the accusation will hang over you, however innocent you are."

Stewart nodded slowly. "I will resign."

"No, you won't. I've got used to you and I don't want another valet. Besides, Lindon expects you to stay."

"With respect, my lord, the other servants won't want me around."

"Fortunately, the other servants do not have a say in the matter. I will speak to Barlow and Mrs. Hicks. Discipline will be maintained."

Stewart searched his eyes. "Thank you," he said with difficulty. "I appreciate your trust."

"Well, you could return it by telling me the truth."

"LADY PETTERIL HAS CALLED."

Just for an instant, the words made no sense to April. Then the meaning hit her like a bucket of water in the face.

Oh, no, not this soon, not when he's not here...

"Show her ladyship into the drawing room," she managed.

"There is no need," came the icy voice of the dowager viscountess, his lordship's aunt Hortensia. "I still remember my way about the house of which I was mistress for thirty years."

The dowager sailed past Mavis, saying grandly, "Be gone, girl."

Mavis, to her credit, actually cast a frightened glance at April to ask if she should obey. April recalled that she had grown to rather like Mavis in their previous relationship and rather feebly wanted to keep her here for moral support. However, she nodded infinitesimally to the girl, who fled with relief, closing the door behind her.

April hoped she would not listen, for whatever the dowager had to say, it was not going to be pleasant.

The dowager stood in the middle of the room, glaring about her. "Where is he?"

"Who, my lady?" asked April, who knew perfectly well, but needed to say something.

"My ingrate idiot of a nephew, of course. Ring for him."

With an effort, April reined in her rising temper. She was no longer the impudent gutter rat, dodging blows and seizing the last word if she thought she could get away with it. She had to prove herself worthy of his lordship.

"Lord Petteril is not at home," she said mildly. She loosened her fierce grip on the book she was holding and laid it on the table. "Please, sit down. Would you like tea?"

"No," the dowager snapped, seating herself in Petteril's chair. "I will wait."

Now what did she do? Her instinct was to pick up her books and carry on with what she had been doing. But that seemed rude. Moreover, some angry, fighting part of herself refused to leave her enemy in possession of the field. She would not be driven out by this woman who had neglected, insulted, and stolen from Lord Petteril. Several withering retorts formed on her lips, but she bit them back.

Instead, she went forward and sat in the chair opposite the dowager, who looked even more outraged. It would have been funny if it wasn't for Petteril. How in the name of God's bottom did one make civil small talk in this situation?

"You need not stay," the dowager snapped. "I shall wait here."

April tried to smile, but this, it seemed, was like a red rag to a bull.

"And you need not sit there looking smug," the dowager spat. "Don't even imagine all this is yours, for it isn't. I'll have this ridiculous marriage annulled and you'll be back out in the gutter where you belong."

"How will you do that?" April asked, not with impudence but because she genuinely wanted to know. It was not something she had thought of, though she expected Petteril had.

The dowager curled her lip. "It is difficult, I grant you, but not impossible when one has connections. I will not allow Piers Withan to sully this family, this name, with such as you. I cannot bear to look at you."

Then don't. Shab off. Again, she swallowed the words. It wasn't difficult this time since she wasn't really angry. This, after all, was the reaction she had expected. Which made the acceptance of the staff even more inexplicable.

Silence stretched. It did not bother April, who had plenty to think about, even if she would rather be doing so while arranging her beautiful, spacious rooms. But it clearly bothered the dowager viscountess, who fumed, sighed and fidgeted in the way April might have done two months ago, before she had learned better.

"Where exactly is he?" the dowager demanded. "When will he be back? Or don't you know?"

"I know he has gone to Lindon Grange. I don't know exactly when he will return but I believe it will be before dinner."

Lady Petteril glared at her, as though more affronted than relieved that she could speak the King's English. April, however, was appalled all over again by the realization that the dowager would have to stay for dinner. She would have to stay the night. The servants would defer to her, not to April. She would do her best to turn them against his lordship, for many of them preceded Piers's succession to the title.

Maybe she should get rid of the woman after all.

April regarded her speculatively. For the first time, a hint of unease stole into the older woman's expression. But before April could take advantage, they were both distracted by the crunch of carriage wheels on the gravel.

Himself, April thought with relief. And yet anxiety remained, worry that she should not have let the old harridan wait to make trouble for him. She hoped he had brought Stewart home...

While she strained her ears for sounds of voices, the dowager shifted in her chair, as though metaphorically rolling up her sleeves to do battle. It seemed she had learned nothing over the preceding months: she still thought she could win against her nephew.

Should she warn him that his aunt was here? No, the servants would tell him before he reached the library. In the midst of the anticipatory silence, she heard his voice, and a lighter, feminine one that was surely familiar.

The door opened and Petteril's cousin Augusta tripped into the room. Gussie was a rather delightful seventeen year old, fresh from her first Season in London. Unlike her mother, she was inherently good-natured if mischievous. She seemed genuinely fond of her cousin Piers, who strolled in behind her and closed the door.

April sprang up, knowing her duties as hostess. "Welcome!" she said, holding out her hand as she crossed the room. "Lady Petteril did not tell me you were here, too."

Gussie smiled with a hint of anxiety but clasped April's hand without hesitation.

Her mother spoke. "I told you to wait in the carriage."

"Oh, Piers saw me and brought me inside."

"Of course I did," Piers said, his gaze locking with April's for an instant. "There is no earthly reason for you to be kept out."

"Oh, isn't there?" the dowager said, bridling. "As her mother, I choose not to have her contaminated by that little gutter brat you are deluded enough to imagine is a suitable viscountess!"

"And yet here you are," Piers said ambiguously. Otherwise ignoring his aunt, he took April's hand and kissed it, a rare enough gesture of affection—in this case probably solidarity —to heat her cheeks.

"Mama!" Gussie whispered in an agony of embarrassment.

"No, I shall not be silent!" The dowager surged to her feet. "How could you, Piers? What possessed you to commit such utter folly? Even you cannot have imagined *that* is a suitable bride, a suitable mother for our heirs? I don't know how she inveigled you into it, but it will not stand. I shall have the marriage discreetly annulled. Until then, for God's sake, send her away. Unthinkable that she should contaminate this place so beloved by my sainted husband and my poor, dead sons."

Piers, retaining April's hand when she would have withdrawn it, turned slowly to face his aunt. This time, you could have cut the silence with a knife. The dowager hadn't produced that tension. Petteril did it, quite deliberately as he gazed at his aunt, not with obvious anger but as though he were examining some strange species.

He had probably learned the skill in a room full of rowdy, arrogant undergraduates, but this was much more refined. This was his role of aloof, haughty viscount, and he had grown into it with a vengeance. Gussie's breath caught.

"Where to even begin to dismantle that monumentally silly farrago?" Piers wondered. "Really, I have only one thing to say. If you wish to remain in this house for the next minute, you will adapt your manners to those of a lady. *Every* respect will be shown to Lady Petteril. If that is beyond you, aunt, you may go. The Red Lion is tolerable, although there is a posting inn about ten miles along the London Road."

The dowager would have spluttered if she could have got her lips close enough together. As it was, she gaped.

At last, a sound broke from her, part cry of fury, part sob of outrage. "How *dare* you speak to me that way, Piers Withan! I am—"

"You are the dowager. *This* is my viscountess. I don't believe either of us invited you, but unless you break the simple rules of hospitality, I shall leave it up to my lady whether or not to accommodate you."

"How can you treat me so," the dowager raged, "when I have saved you from the ridicule of the world?"

Petteril, in the act of turning to April, paused and gazed back at his aunt, searching her face. For the first time since he had entered the room, April sensed anxiety.

"Aunt, what have you done?" he asked softly.

Chapter Three

Aunt Hortensia sensed her moment of victory, for she drew herself up to her full height. "I? I have taken care of this family as I have done for thirty years. While you have proved yourself constitutionally incapable at every turn."

"Specifically, aunt."

"When you sent your note informing me of your marriage, you did not tell me the name of your bride. But Bertie did."

"Soliciting Mama's kindness for your wife," Gussie interpolated, anxious, no doubt, to acquit Bertie of betrayal.

"At least he had the courage," Aunt Hortensia said, looking Piers up and down with the same contempt she always had.

"I was not hiding it, aunt," Piers said mildly. "So, what did you do?"

"I told a few friends that she was an heiress you had met abroad. Now, it's what everyone thinks."

Including the staff, who just hadn't looked carefully enough, although they would in time and despise April even more for the lie. More than that, April's only condition to their marriage had been honesty. Now, Aunt Hortensia's interference had taken that away, and the fact that Piers himself had suggested a similar kind of plan to April in the beginning, added to his shame.

Beside him, she had gone very still. And opposite them, Aunt Hortensia looked positively triumphant.

"We may spin another yarn," she said regally. "Once this ridiculous marriage is annulled."

Rare anger flared inside him, along with the inevitable, familiar fear of life getting away from him, just as he was making a leap towards...

But he could not give into melancholy. He had a wife to care for, responsibilities to fulfil.

"I can't believe I have to repeat this," he said slowly. "There will be no annulment. I am not ashamed of my wife and neither should you be. There will be no lies told here." Except by omission, it seemed. "Nor will I have you meddling in my affairs. Is that clear?"

"You imbecile, who will—"

"*Is that clear?*" His own voice thundered in his ears, taking everyone by surprise. He never shouted.

"Perfectly!" said the dowager stiffly. For a moment, he thought she would fight him, but then she did not risk it. Perhaps it was good to shout occasionally.

He was almost afraid to look at April. But she met his gaze, her eyes so veiled that his heart sank. Still, he asked with a flicker of his eyebrow, and she answered with a definite nod.

"Lady Petteril has a larger heart than I," he pronounced, walking toward the bell and tugging it. "She is prepared to overlook your insulting words and invite you to dine and stay for the night at Haybury Court. It will not be convenient for you to stay longer."

The door opened and one of the footmen appeared. Blond. It was Patrick.

"Bring in my aunt's baggage and have the carriage sent around to the stables. And inform Mrs. Hicks that my aunt and cousin will dine with us tonight and stay overnight."

"Yes, my lord."

"Let me show you to your rooms," April said, walking to the door.

Piers was proud of her. Her very courtesy, cool as it was, showed up Hortensia's manners as deplorable. He wished Hortensia could see that, though he didn't hold out much hope.

"Come, Mama." Gussie took her mother's arm, as though afraid she was going to resist, and tugged her after April.

Silence surrounded Piers. He sank with relief into April's vacated chair. "Welcome home, Withan," he murmured. He hadn't expected it to be easy, but to face April's first day as lady of Haybury, the accusation of theft against his valet, and his aunt's malicious mischief all at once was something of a challenge.

God knew how April was feeling.

APRIL, IN FACT, WAS less angry than she knew his lordship to be. Although annoyed with the dowager for interfering and spoiling things, she recognized all too easily the truth behind her insults.

April was not a fit wife for Lord Petteril. He should by right have married a beautiful, kind, clever lady of his own class, who knew how to look after his house and servants and tenants. Who understood her role of wife and chatelaine to a nobleman and could bear him children without the stigma of low birth.

But things didn't always go according to plan—or Piers would have remained a happy, obscure academic while his cousin inherited the viscountcy. And she would never have met Petteril again after burgling his house. But she had and they were friends, such friends that on that day in Lisbon, when he had proposed marriage, she had seen clearly that she—perhaps only she—could make him happy.

By then, her own happiness was so bound to him that she had grasped the chance. Who wouldn't?

At the top of the stairs, she turned left. Lady Petteril, presumably thinking April did not yet know her own house, turned right toward the family apartments.

"This way, if you please," April said pleasantly.

"I have no intention of sleeping in the guest wing."

"You do not have to sleep," April said before she could stop herself. Hastily, she added, "Two of the guest bedchambers have been refurbished, unlike most of the family apartments. You will be more comfortable here."

She did not wait for them. From the sounds behind her, she imagined Gussie was towing her mother along. April's lips twitched.

She opened the door on her right. "For you, my lady. I hope you will be comfortable. The footman will be up with your bags directly, but ring if you need anything. Dinner will be at seven. Miss Withan, you are next door..."

Gussie hastily shut her mother's bedchamber door on her mother's uttered, "Upstart...!"

"You are quite right," Gussie said with desperate gaiety. "That room is lovely."

"Here you are." April opened the next door along the passage.

"Goodness, how pretty." Gussie swept inside, gazing admiringly around her.

April turned to go.

"You're very kind," Gussie added, forcing her to turn back. The girl's face was anxious, a little ashamed. "I-I am sorry about Mama. She has very fixed ideas and she has not yet come to terms with the fact that Piers is viscount. Look, I'm honestly stunned that he married you. Unless you are a princess in disguise—"

April laughed.

"But I am your friend," Gussie said seriously, "for whatever that is worth."

April smiled. "A good deal."

Gussie smiled back with just a hint of shyness, quite rare in her. "You're different."

"Because I have adjusted my accent? I may wear silk, but I am still the sow's ear."

"You are Piers's wife."

April inclined her head. "I am. I'll see you at dinner, Miss Withan."

"Call me Gussie."

"Your mama wouldn't like it."

Gussie sighed. "Well, she won't like me to call you Lady Petteril either, so let us agree on Gussie and April. After all, we're cousins now."

Thoughtfully, April made her way back to her own apartments. She would have gone to fetch the books she had chosen, but she expected that, like her, Lord Petteril needed a moment's quiet.

So she drew one of the comfortable chairs in front of the window and curled up in it with the novel she had been reading. It was difficult to concentrate, though after a little, she realized the sheer space, light, and beauty of the room surrounding her was oddly soothing. As was the view from the window, and the scents of late summer that filled the room—fresh, country smells that had once seemed so alien to her. Lord Petteril had said it was harvest time, so there would be much to learn.

Then there was the matter of poor Stewart. They would need to get to the bottom of that. Perhaps she should go and talk to him. She did not doubt that his lordship had brought him home.

She laid aside the book, then paused. She was Lady Petteril now. She could go anywhere she chose, but she had been in enough servants' halls to know that an unplanned invasion by the mistress was resented. Should she ring the bell and ask whoever came to send Stewart to her? That was what Petteril would do.

As she rose, a knock sounded at the door, and she froze with foolish unease, reaching for the role of haughty Lady Petteril. Perhaps the servants had finally worked out why she looked so familiar.

Good, she told herself firmly. "Come in."

But it was Lord Petteril who entered the room, kicking the door closed behind him, for his arms were full of books. Rushing to unburden him of a few, she was rather touched that he still knocked—a habit begun for decency's sake when they travelled incognito to Portugal pretending to be man and wife.

"I assumed you wanted these brought up here," he said, bending to deposit the rest of the pile on the floor beside the bookcase. April put the few she had relieved him of on the bottom shelf, and they both rose together.

He stood close, gazing down at her, that faint, continual frown between his brows once more. It had almost disappeared while they roamed Portugal.

"I'm sorry," he said. "I never thought of her storming in the day of our arrival. And you had to face her alone."

"I was very good and polite. Not sure you were."

"I won't tolerate her disrespect to you."

"We knew it would happen," April said philosophically. "She won't be the only one."

"It will not happen in this house. That, at least, I can do for you. Though I never imagined her inventing stories to explain you."

April drew in her breath. If she didn't ask him now, she never would. "Then why did you not tell her whom you had married?" She was rather pleased with the *whom*. "Why did you not tell the staff?"

The veil came down over his eyes and he moved away. As always, she was disappointed.

"Mostly," he said restlessly, "because it was not their business. The staff needed to know I was bringing home a bride. As a courtesy, I wrote to my aunt. It seemed enough."

"Only mostly?"

"I didn't really think about it at the time. It was natural to write as briefly as I did. Now, I wonder if I wasn't unconsciously putting it off—not from shame, before you even think it, but as if...if *we* didn't think about trouble, there would not *be* any. And now there is."

"Never mind. She'll be gone tomorrow. And Gussie is kind. She seems prepared to be friends, whoever I am."

As she spoke, she began to drag the other chair to the window. Lord Petteril brushed her aside and moved it for her. They both sat down and his gaze roved around the room. Was there an awkwardness between them now? She couldn't bear that.

"How is Stewart?"

"He is well, physically. Lindon gave him up without much of a fight, but then there was no evidence either, except that he went upstairs to support his friend who was bosky and deposited him in his room. And there are several minutes unaccounted for between him leaving his friend and reappearing in the taproom."

"What was he doing during those minutes?"

"Sitting on the stairs in contemplation." Petteril's eyes came back to her, his frown more pronounced than ever. "He's lying. Or at least, not telling me the full truth and I can't shift him."

"You don't believe he *did* take the money, do you?" April asked uneasily.

Petteril shook his head. "It's beneath him. Besides, the purse could have been stolen any time between its owner—one Sir Darius Camden—going down to the taproom on Tuesday evening and noticing its absence from his room the following day. If indeed it was stolen at all and isn't languishing under the bed for the maid to find once the room is vacated."

April thought about it. "Perhaps Stewart is covering for his friend? Who is he?"

"Fellow called Neil Murray whom he knew in Scotland."

"A good friend?"

"It would seem so, since he took the trouble to meet him. Only..."

"What?" April asked.

"It struck me Stewart didn't like him very much."

"Well, Stewart doesn't like anyone very much. Doesn't stop him being loyal."

"As we both have cause to know," Petteril agreed.

"Is Mr. Lindon going to investigate the matter properly? Or will we have to?"

Petteril's lip quirked upward. "Oh, I think we'll do that anyway, don't you?"

April smiled with relief, awkwardness vanishing because some things never changed. "Not today, though," she said with regret. "We have guests and I need to dress again."

"They're heating water for baths as we speak."

She wriggled with delight. Definitely, there were pleasures to being Lady Petteril.

His lordship rose. "In fact, I shall leave you. Come and find me when you are ready, and we can go down to dinner together."

His support was appreciated. But she would have preferred his company now.

PIERS WAS, IN FACT, driven from his wife's side by the talk of baths. And her unconsciously sensual little wriggle. There were limits to restraint, even for a man of honour, which he was trying desperately hard to be.

"Oh," he recalled from her doorway. "I have summoned the servants to the reception room before dinner. We need to announce our belief in Stewart or his position will become untenable."

"Of course."

Perhaps, he reflected as he made his way to his own rooms, they shouldn't bother heating water for him. A cold bath seemed to be more in order.

He found Stewart in his rooms, once more his clean, immaculate self, unpacking Piers's trunk and putting everything away in its proper place.

"I've spoken to Barlow and Mrs. Hicks," Piers said. "They will assemble the servants in the reception room where Lady Petteril and I will address them. You will be with us."

"Yes, my lord." Stewart hesitated. "I have not even congratulated you on your marriage yet. I wish you every happiness."

"Thank you, Stewart," he said briskly.

An hour later, duly bathed and resplendent in a black evening coat and pure white cravat with a jet and gold pin, he hung his quizzing glasses around his neck and nodded to the viscount gazing back at him from the mirror. He no longer seemed quite so unfamiliar.

A knock at the sitting room door sent him in that direction, but Stewart was already walking toward it. Curiously, Piers hung back, watching.

Stewart opened the door and April breezed in. His eyes widened slightly, but that was all.

"Good evening, Mr. Stewart," she said in her perfect accent, although her eyes twinkled as though inviting him to share the joke.

"Good evening, my lady," he replied.

"Hmm, you don't look very surprised," she said.

"I'm not. I was at the Queen's Head."

She gave him one of her dazzling smiles which caught audibly at Stewart's breath and silently at Piers's.

"Is it a secret?" Stewart asked evenly.

"No," April said. "Though you seem to be the first to recognize me. I'm very glad to see you again."

"I'm sorry for the...trouble," Stewart said.

"Oh, we'll fix that," April said cheerfully. "Is his lordship—oh, there you are," she finished, catching sight of Piers. She looked him up and down. "The perfect viscount."

Piers accorded her the same survey. She wore blue silk and pearls, striking just the right note between fashionable elegance and modesty. She had been learning to dress her own hair and had made an excellent job of the simple yet becoming style.

"And the perfect viscountess," he managed. "Your appearance should give even my aunt pause. Shall we?"

He offered her his arm, which she took without fuss. She smelled of fresh, clean soap and flowers he couldn't name.

Stewart opened the door for them and followed.

On the ground floor, a hum of chatter drifted from the large reception room, though it cut off like a tap as soon as Piers and April entered.

Barlow swished one hand for silence, but his underlings had already stopped talking. Everyone bowed or curtseyed. Stewart emerged from behind Piers and went and stood with the other servants, where he received a few sideways glances.

Piers had thought quite carefully about the best way to address them and exactly what he should say to both quell suspicion where Stewart was concerned and ensure obedience, without making the issue appear so huge that they would feel obliged to look for other positions. Not that there were any better in the area.

"Thank you for taking the time in the midst of your busiest part of the day," Piers said, keeping his voice mild. "We shall not keep you long. We rejoice to see Stewart back among us with this unpleasant misunderstanding cleared up. On this subject, I know Mrs. Hicks and Barlow have already explained that Stewart was released without charge. Any accusation of theft is serious, so Lady Petteril and I wish you to be sure that our trust in Stewart is as high as ever. As is our trust in all of you."

He let his gaze linger on each face as he spoke, making sure they understood the link he was making. The misfortune of suspicion could fall on any domestic servant, even one as senior as his lordship's valet, and therefore the trust of the master and mistress was vital.

He addressed Cookie, as she had been known in his childhood, picking her out by her age and dress rather than by her face. "Mrs. Drake, I'm sure you'll agree the poor man needs feeding up after his nasty ordeal, so I hope you've made him something special."

Cookie beamed. "We've already eaten, but I've saved him back a bit of yours just for once!"

Piers glanced at April who hastily said, "Excellent," and bestowed one of her sunny smiles on Cookie. The woman looked startled.

Piers said, "Just before you return to your duties, reading and writing lessons will resume in the library tomorrow morning for interested parties. Thank you."

Before he turned to open the door, he noticed one of the outside servants gazing rather fixedly at April. From his age and dress, Piers recognized Benson, the groom he had employed in London, who had known April when she was merely Ape the urchin, learning to care for horses.

"I think that passed off tolerably well," Piers said as they crossed the hall to the staircase.

"Just right, I think. Though we'd better hurry and find the wretched purse before Mr. Lindon comes back for Stewart."

"Indeed. On to the next hurdle."

They walked upstairs to the dining room, but before they reached it, he glimpsed his aunt through the drawing room door. Exchanging glances with April, he changed direction.

In the drawing room, his aunt sat straight-backed on the edge of a chair. Gussie, looking horribly embarrassed, was on the sofa opposite.

"You must have changed the staff," Aunt Hortensia greeted him. "No one came when I rang."

"I'm afraid there was no one to hear in the last five minutes," Piers said, refusing to apologize. The clock on the mantelpiece told him it was still not quite seven. "We have been addressing the staff. Did you require anything in particular? A glass of sherry or ratafia, perhaps?"

"I loathe ratafia. You should know that."

"Should I?" Piers said vaguely, going to the decanters. "Have some sherry, then."

As he brought the glasses over, he was glad to see April had sat beside Gussie. Most open and friendly of his cousins, her friendship could only help smooth April's difficult way ahead.

"Do tell us about your wedding journey," Gussie said brightly. "What is Portugal like? And Bertie said you were actually married in Spain!"

"What on earth were you even doing there?" Aunt Hortensia asked with a frown. "You could have done no good at all looking for Bertie."

"On the contrary, it was Lord Petteril who did find him," April said. "And I loved Portugal. Everything is so much brighter there. It even smells different."

Aunt Hortensia sniffed. "How was Bertie when you left him?"

"In pretty good health, considering," Piers said. "And eager to see action."

It was the wrong thing to say, of course. Bertie was very much Hortensia's favourite nephew—inevitably since Piers was now the only other—and she did not want him anywhere near military action.

Fortunately, Barlow announced that dinner was served, and they all repaired to the dining room for an excruciating meal.

"You should have kept my cook," Aunt Hortensia said.

Piers sighed. "I did."

This was the first dinner at which April had acted as hostess. She knew she was supposed to lead the ladies back to the drawing room at some point, leaving Piers in solitary possession of the dining room and the port. But she was nervous and unsure of the precise timing, covertly watching the progress of Hortensia and Gussie through their sweet pastries and fruit and cheese.

Conversation, already stilted in front of the servants, though at least it kept Hortensia mostly civil, had almost dried up.

Below the table, Piers touched April's foot with his. She sprang up just a little too quickly.

"Shall we withdraw, ladies?" she said.

A spasm crossed Hortensia's face. Clearly, she felt her place usurped, not only by a wife of Piers's, but by one she did not consider worthy of the role. It was all nonsense, of course. Even before April had married him, she had already done more for the people of Haybury than Hortensia had done in her whole life. This was the first time in probably ten years she had been near the place.

As the ladies departed, Piers silently wished his wife luck. Barlow placed the port and the brandy decanters before him, along with a fresh glass, then bowed and departed. As soon as the door closed behind him, Piers stood.

He would not leave April to suffer alone for long, but first, he was in sore need of fresh air.

Chapter Four

U sing the west staircase, he left the house by a side door and walked straight toward the moss covered ruin which rose on its own mound, silhouetted against the moonlit sky. It was a very Gothic ruin, clearly the romantic remains of a medieval chapel, damaged in war or religious zeal, now overgrown with centuries of neglect.

Only it wasn't. It had been built just like this about seventy years ago by another eccentric viscount who wanted to add character to his grounds. Even the grass and flowers had been deliberately grown among the stones.

It had been known as the Viscount's Folly. Perhaps for that reason, Piers had rediscovered its appeal during his last visit. He had used to come here as a boy, too, making up stories in his head as if it had been truly medieval, until his brother and cousins had spoiled the game.

Tonight, he had no time to sit and daydream. He meant only to walk once around it and return to the house to join April in the drawing room. But someone had beaten him to it.

Annoyed, Piers was about to change direction to avoid the company of whoever sat on the low, stone wall, until he thought he recognized the shape of the intruder. He went closer, climbing the mound.

Oddly, Stewart's face was one he generally recognized without difficulty. Like April's. There must be something else about each of them, he thought, that identified them in his wayward brain.

Clearly deep in thought, Stewart did not notice Piers's approach until he was almost upon him. Then he sprang up, startled, as though caught in some dereliction of duty.

35

"How was it?" Piers asked casually.

"I haven't been driven out of the servants' hall," Stewart said sardonically. "I just wanted a moment. I like it here."

It struck Piers that Stewart's recent predilection for moments alone, such as on the stairs of the Red Lion, were what had got him into trouble in the first place. Something was troubling his valet, something more than a wrongful accusation which could not be proved.

Piers stepped over the wall and found his own favourite stone below the empty window. Questioning Stewart hadn't won his trust. So he waited.

Stewart drew in his breath. "Thank you for what you said this evening. I believe it made all the difference." He rose, bowed, and walked back to the house, leaving Piers frowning after him.

APRIL HAD NOT GOT AS far as the drawing room before the dowager said coldly, "We shall not trouble you further but bid you good night."

"Mama!" Gussie protested. Lifting her chin she said, "I would enjoy a cup of tea with Cousin April."

"No," said Hortensia, narrowing her eyes at her daughter, "you would not. We are tired after our journey. Good night."

Gussie looked unhappy, but with a quick, apologetic smile at April, followed her mother to the staircase.

At least they said good night, April thought philosophically. And truth be known, she was excessively glad to be out of Hortensia's stifling company. Now, at last, she was free to do what she had wished to all day. She slipped out of the front door and followed the dark path around to the stables.

Only as she arrived did she realize she was most unsuitably attired in her evening gown. But at least the grooms and stable lads appeared to have retired. Only one lantern still glowed, hung on the inner stable wall. A low murmur issued from within, making April smile. She knew who it was.

She walked into the stable, breathing in the smell of horse and leather. "Evening, Mr. Benson."

Benson, in the process of delivering a last treat to each of the horses, spun around. For an instant, the warmth of pleasure lit his face, hastily replaced by a wariness that hurt April, even though she had known it would happen. By marrying his lordship, she had ended a number of relationships that were important to her.

Benson bowed. "My lady. How can I serve you?"

She swallowed. "I just came to see the horses. And you."

Several of the horses whickered at the scent of her and she went around stroking the noses of each, letting them blow into her neck: Lady, the good-natured mare Petteril had begun teaching her to ride; the Professor, his favourite riding horse; the smart, beautiful matching greys who pulled his curricle when he drove himself; Orion, the old hunter.

Once, her greatest ambition had been to look after these horses as a stable lad.

"I know things have to be different now," she blurted. "But I'm still your friend and I'm still grateful."

"There's no cause for that," Benson said gruffly. "I'm glad for you. Flabbergasted, but glad for you."

She had to smile at him for that. Before she cried, she said, "How have they been?"

"Missing his lordship—and you, truth be told—but they're in fine condition. Even Orion there. The new lad's been riding him out every day." Benson held out the rest of his treats, and April took them, happily feeding them to the greedy horses.

She didn't stay long. She knew it wouldn't be right for either her or Benson. So she flitted out again with no more than a "Good night."

Still restless, she veered off the path until she could see the ruin known as the folly. A bizarre structure with no use, built by a man with too much time and money on his hands. She paused, then, for someone was there.

Lord Petteril. Piers. Her husband.

Had he come here to be alone?

As if he sensed her presence, he turned his head and saw her. He smiled. Her heart always swelled to see that rare smile—rarer again now that they had returned to England. She walked up and sat beside him, nudging his arm as he often did hers.

"All well?" she asked lightly.

"Mostly. Stewart worries me." He blinked, as though reminding himself of the last time he had seen her. "Free already? Was she awful?"

"No. She was obliging enough to retire rather than join me in the drawing room."

"Hmm."

"Did I do—did I behave correctly?"

"Very correctly, which is more than I can say for my aunt. You're coping wonderfully well and in trying circumstances."

Basking in his praise, she enjoyed the silent companionship for several minutes.

"You must be cold," he said, as though suddenly noticing she wore nothing over her evening dress.

She shook her head. She remembered very well what cold felt like and it wasn't this. But he removed his coat anyway and placed it around her shoulders. She couldn't help liking his solicitude, his courtesy. And the light, too-brief touch of his hands.

"Shall we go to the inn tomorrow?" he said.

"I think that would be best." Her voice felt hoarse with relief that he was including her. Not that she would have accepted *ex*clusion, but this was definitely better.

He rose, casually holding out his hand as though she were a lady frail enough to need help getting to her feet. The novelty still pleased her, so she took his hand and walked with him, and he didn't immediately release her.

She liked that too, walking with him hand-in-hand, like children. Like sweethearts.

One day...

FROM HIS LORDSHIP'S bedchamber window, Stewart saw his master and new mistress walking close together. She wore Lord Petteril's coat about her shoulders, and Stewart suspected their fingers were joined though he couldn't be sure.

It gave him enough warning to be wary the following morning, when he once more entered his lordship's apartments. Lord Petteril did not care to be dressed and undressed – like a baby, as he put it. He preferred to look after himself and leave Stewart to care for his clothes, his rooms and his comfort. Therefore, Stewart had got into the habit of leaving him a cup of coffee in his sitting room. Sometimes it was drunk; sometimes, when his lordship was already riding out even earlier than usual, it was not.

Stewart found the sitting room empty. His sensitive nostrils picked up no scent of April. Lady Petteril. He was just setting down the cup when the bedchamber door opened, and his lordship strode out in his riding clothes.

"Good morning, Stewart," he said cheerfully, and grasped at the coffee cup. "Her ladyship and I are riding out, but we should be back in time for breakfast."

"Very good, my lord. I'll make sure Mr. Barlow and Cook are aware."

Lord Petteril drank down more than half the cup, then strode off.

Taking the opportunity to tidy, Stewart picked up his lordship's casually abandoned evening coat and took it through to the dressing room before going to sort out the gentle chaos normally left behind in the bedchamber.

Only one side of the bed had been slept in.

Which was just as it should be, of course. In the aristocratic world, gentlemen tended not to linger with their wives. Still, Stewart was surprised. The viscount was not much like other noblemen and from the sight of the couple last night...well, they were newly married.

With a few practised tugs and folds, Stewart tidied the sheets, plumped the pillows, and spread up the coverlet.

If he was ever privileged to have a wife, Stewart would spend every moment he could in her bed. He cut off the thought there and refused to think about Petteril's private affairs either. He had enough on his mind. And much of it was shame.

APRIL ENJOYED THE RIDE over to the Red Lion with Lord Petteril. Unexpectedly, she felt a kind of homecoming to see all the familiar places again, the woods, the farmhouses, the village...

The few people they encountered all called greetings or tugged their caps. Some came closer, she was sure, merely to gawp at the new viscountess. She wondered how long it would take them to recognize her in her fashionable new riding habit.

Barnes, the landlord, bowed obsequiously to them both. He had barely glanced at April in the past, but her ladyship was clearly worth more respect.

"Just coffee, if you please," Petteril ordered. "And a quick word with you when you have a moment."

"Of course, my lord!"

Barnes brought their coffee himself to the otherwise empty common room and poured it for them. April used the time to look around.

The coffee room was the inn's central area, including as it did the front door and the staircase to the upper floor and the bedchambers. Through a door to the left of the coffee room, currently closed, was the taproom.

From the taproom, with the door open, one would be able to see who went up and down the stairs. But would the door not have been closed to muffle the taproom noise from the bedchambers above? She supposed there would be no need if all the guests were in the taproom anyway. And if Stewart's friend was bosky enough to need help to his room, he would have been out like a light anyway.

Petteril waved the innkeeper to the seat opposite, and Barnes sat looking expectant while April sipped her coffee.

"This business of the theft," Petteril began.

Barnes immediately adopted a grave expression. "Never thought such of anyone who worked for your lordship."

"Good," said Petteril briskly, "because it's as plain as the nose on your face that he didn't do it. Is the victim of the theft still staying here?"

"Oh yes, my lord. He and his sister. He has a head cold and doesn't want to move on until it's better."

"And he still has not found his purse?"

"No, my lord," Barnes sighed.

"I take it," Petteril said delicately, "that his room has been searched for it?"

"Oh yes, my lord. Sir Darius and Miss Camden, his sister, rifled through all his things, and the maids checked under beds and inside cupboards. The purse is definitely not there."

"Hmmm. I understand the door is lockable. Did Sir Darius always lock it when he left?"

Barnes scratched his head. "You mean, did he lock it before he came down to the taproom? That I could not swear to. He says he always did, and certainly Verity—our maidservant—has always had to unlock the door when she goes in to make the bed and tidy up."

"Who else would have a key to that room?"

"Just me and the wife. The maids use her set of keys to get into the rooms to clean."

"Where are the keys kept," April asked, "when they're not needed?"

Barnes swept aside his apron to show a large ring of keys dangling from his belt. "My wife wears her set, too, except when she gives it to the maids for morning cleaning."

"And what sort of time do they clean?" Petteril asked.

"Oh very early for the unoccupied rooms. The others are cleaned whenever it's convenient or when a guest departs."

"I see. So no maid had gone into Sir Darius's room before he realized his purse was missing?"

"No, of course not," Barnes said, clearly affronted. "My staff is honest."

"Of course they are," Petteril said amiably. "Just like mine."

Barnes flushed. "Speaking personally, my lord, I always found Mr. Stewart very civil and polite, and you could have knocked me down with a feather when I heard he'd been taken up for the theft. But I could only say the truth about what I saw."

"Which was what exactly?"

"That Mr. Stewart went upstairs with Mr. Murray and came back to the taproom about ten minutes later to fetch his hat. He said goodnight and off he went. Last I thought about it until next morning when Sir Darius starts yelling blue murder and we had to tear the place apart to find his purse."

"What happened during the rest of that evening?" April asked, frowning. "After Stewart had left. Did no one else go upstairs during that time?"

"Only the guests to go to bed. Sir Darius himself and Captain Lyall."

"Ah, who is Captain Lyall?" Petteril asked.

"*There* is Captain Lyall," Barnes said as an uneven footfall sounded on the stairs. "Wounded officer back from the war. Making his way home to his family in easy stages. He'll be wanting his breakfast. If you would excuse me."

"Of course," Petteril said. "Perhaps you would introduce us?"

"Yes, my lord," Barnes said with unexpected doubt. "Though he don't say much." He rose to his feet.

"One more thing, Mr. Barnes," April said. "Did any of the staff go upstairs at all that evening? To serve your guests or go to bed, or for any other reason?"

"No. Tucker the tapster goes home to the village. Verity the maid uses the outside stairs to the attic. My lady."

He bowed and scurried off to greet his guest, a tall, terribly thin and pale man in a worn, dark green uniform coat. He leaned heavily on a walking stick. And one empty sleeve was pinned to his shoulder.

Apart from Barnes's initial greeting, April could not hear the conversation, although the soldier did glance in their direction, his frown deepening. Then he shrugged and limped toward them. Barnes leapt to introduce them.

"This is Captain Lyall, my lord," he said hurriedly. "Captain, Lord and Lady Petteril."

The soldier gave a brief, not terribly reverent bow—more of a nod, really.

Lord Petteril waved his hand to the chair opposite. "Care to join us? We are just back from the Peninsula ourselves."

The captain's expression was not quite blatant disbelief, though his lips twisted into a smile. "You appear to have survived the experience better than I."

He sat down and propped his stick against the table.

"Well, mere civilian travellers, you know," Petteril said.

Not unnaturally, the captain cast him a curious look as though wondering why a nobleman, expensively dressed with no fewer than two quizzing glasses dangling at his chest, would choose to travel in war-torn countries, especially with his wife in tow.

Petteril did not enlighten him, which probably piqued the man's interest.

"Rifle Brigade," Petteril observed, nodding to the uniform. "We met some of your fellows in Spain."

"*Formerly* Rifle Brigade. My war is ended."

Petteril nodded without obvious sympathy. "One door closes," he said vaguely. "Another opens."

Captain Lyall's disinterested gaze came back to him, as though wondering whether he was being crass. He couldn't know that Lord Petteril's experience of life was similar, if somewhat less traumatic. He hadn't found that open door easily, but he had walked through it and April was proud of him.

She wondered who would be proud of Captain Lyall.

Barnes brought him coffee and promised breakfast directly. Lyall nodded curtly by way of thanks, but otherwise looked uninterested.

"I'm hoping you can help us," Petteril said apologetically. "I expect you've heard my man was arrested for the theft of Sir Darius's purse."

"I did hear something."

"He's released, of course. No evidence against him. But the affair bothers me. I'd like to get to the bottom of it."

Lyall raised his eyebrows. "Why?"

"Curiosity. My besetting sin."

"I don't see how I can help," Lyall said, "but you may ask."

"You were in the taproom that evening, I believe. Did you see Stewart—my valet—there?"

"I didn't know who they were, but I noticed two well-dressed men in earnest conversation. One of them is still at the inn. Can't remember his name."

"I expect you saw them leave the taproom together."

"Holding each other up."

"Holding each other?" Petteril repeated. "It wasn't Stewart supporting his friend?"

Lyall shrugged. "I wasn't paying attention. I just noticed them leave." His frown deepened again. "Very close together. I thought they were holding each other up but they weren't happy drunks. They were annoyed with each other."

"How do you know that?" Petteril pounced.

The captain's lips twisted again. "I've been in the company of a great number of men over the last four years. Men who depend on each other. I read them well enough."

"I imagine you do," Petteril said thoughtfully. "And how long was it before you saw Stewart again?"

"Couldn't say. A few minutes.

"Two or three? Ten or fifteen?"

"Something like that." Lyall met Petteril's gaze with a hint of mockery. "Not entirely sober myself. Thank you," he added as Mrs. Barnes placed before him a steaming plate of ham, sausages, beef, mushrooms, and eggs.

Beaming, she set a smaller plate of fresh bread and toasted bread at his elbow and a large slab of butter. "Eat up, captain, sir. Good food works wonders. Welcome my lord. My lady."

She curtseyed to them, her avid gaze drinking in Petteril and April before lingering on her.

"Thank you, Mrs. Barnes. Very glad to be home," Piers assured her. "I trust you're well?"

"Oh yes, my lord, thanks for asking!"

April wasn't sure how he did it, but somehow, his look dismissed the innkeeper's curious wife.

"Anyone else go up or down the stairs while you were in the taproom?" Petteril asked Lyall without much hope.

"Not that I noticed." The captain, having hacked a rasher of bacon into three pieces, laid down his knife and picked up his fork. He prodded the bacon onto his fork, ferried it to his mouth and chewed without enthusiasm.

"Did you notice who was serving that night?" Petteril asked.

Lyall swallowed some coffee as though to wash down the remains of his bacon. "Barnes and the lad—Tucker? The maidservant too. Verity. Mrs. Barnes was mostly in the kitchen, the girl scurrying between."

April leaned forward. "Was the door to the taproom open or closed?"

Both men turned to her as though surprised.

"Good point," Lord Petteril said. "It should have been closed, shouldn't it? In which case how would any of you have seen who went up and down the stairs?"

Chapter Five

Lyall took the trouble to think about it, clearly seeing the importance.

"Actually, the door *was* closed some of the time," he recalled. Almost mechanically he forked another piece of bacon and egg. "But whenever anyone went in or out, it tended to get left open—like when your man and his friend staggered out, or Verity brought in food from the kitchen."

While he ate, April and Petteril exchanged glances. Perhaps the inn's patrons couldn't have gone upstairs unnoticed, but the staff could have. Which proved nothing, except that Stewart was not the only person who could have possibly stolen the purse while its owner was in the taproom.

"Thank you, Captain," April said. "You've been very helpful."

His eyes widened. For a moment, his general air of disinterest was replaced with curiosity. "I have?"

"Indeed," Petteril said. "If..." He trailed off as Lyall's attention—and his own—were distracted by the sight of a young lady descending the stairs with purposeful speed. She was possibly a few years older than April—five-and-twenty, perhaps—her gown of good quality fabric but cut without being terribly fashionable. April could judge these things now, to some degree. The lady's soft brown hair was simply dressed, though its few escaping strands told April she had pinned it herself. Her face was pleasing, full of character more than obvious prettiness.

"Good morning, Captain," she said cheerfully. "Is Mrs. Barnes in the vicinity?"

Mrs. Barnes emerged from the back of the house as though on cue. "Yes, Miss Camden? Will you have breakfast upstairs or down? Lady Petteril is here, so you need not fear being unchaperoned."

Petteril rose to his feet. So, with more awkwardness, did Lyall, grasping the table as he levered himself up. April had to remind herself—again—that she no longer needed to rise in the presence of a lady.

"That is not something I have ever feared, Mrs. Barnes," the lady said wryly.

"This is Miss Camden," Captain Lyall said in his curt way. "Ma'am, Lord and Lady Petteril."

Miss Camden curtseyed without looking over-impressed. "How do you do? Please be seated, gentlemen. I shan't stay."

"How is Sir Darius this morning?" Mrs. Barnes inquired.

Miss Camden's eyes twinkled. "He seems better to me but like many active men with a cold, he is convinced he is at death's door. May we have breakfast in his chamber? I might as well try to cheer him up!"

"Perhaps you would ask him," Lord Petteril said diffidently, moving toward her, "if he is up to receiving a visitor while he waits for his breakfast? Here is my card."

Miss Camden gazed at him in some surprise before she took the card. "Thank you. I shall give it to him directly." As she turned back to the stairs, the quick, interrogative glance she cast at Captain Lyall was not lost on April. Nor was the very faint hint of colour seeping into his pallid cheeks.

Lyall sat back down and speared a mushroom with unexpected force. April sipped her coffee. Petteril wandered about and gazed out of the window.

Miss Camden was not long. Leaning over the banister, she called, "Lord Petteril? My brother is happy to receive you if you are prepared to risk infection."

"I must screw my courage to the sticking point," Petteril said. "You will excuse me, my dear," he added to April and followed Miss Camden back upstairs.

April surprised a gleam of amusement in Captain Lyall's eyes as he pushed his food about the plate.

"Will you stay long at the Red Lion, captain?" she asked.

"As long as I can get away with."

"You are avoiding going home?" she guessed.

"I am."

"Because you will have to think what to do with the rest of your life without the army?"

He laid his knife and fork together on his still full plate. "Something like that."

"I hope you will call on us before you go. We are at Haybury Court. Barnes will arrange a vehicle if you are not up to riding."

"I can ride," he said at once.

"Then come to tea. Or drink wine with Petteril."

He regarded her with bafflement. "Thank you. Perhaps I will. Would you excuse me? If you don't mind being left alone."

"Not in the slightest. Good day, Captain Lyall."

"My lady." He bowed and limped out of the door.

Only moments later, Miss Camden came down. "It is cramped in there with three of us," she told April, "so I am leaving them alone."

"Join me," April invited.

"Has Captain Lyall gone for his daily constitutional?"

"He certainly went out. He doesn't eat much, does he?"

"I think he is in a great deal of pain still." Miss Camden regarded her with open curiosity. "Lord Petteril told my brother he is trying to find his missing purse. Grateful as we are, is that not rather eccentric behaviour for a viscount?"

"Not for this one. He is an eccentric viscount."

"Excellent," said the surprising Miss Camden. "I always prefer eccentric people. The conventional tend to look at me askance because I prefer to travel with my eccentric brother rather than settle down to marriage and children."

"Where do you travel to?"

"Wherever our noses take us. We have been all over the British Isles, hunting botanical specimens. Darius is an amateur botanist."

What the devil is a botanist? April wondered in panic. Then she remembered some large, beautifully illustrated books in Petteril's library. *Plants. Sir Darius is a plants man.*

"Do you share his interest?" April asked.

"Only in a very limited way. I find people more interesting than plants."

"I wish you had been in the taproom on Wednesday evening, then. I'm sure you would have noted a great deal more than Stewart, Barnes and Captain Lyall did between them."

Her eyes laughed. "My dear Lady Petteril. A lady in a taproom? I would truly be beyond the pale."

"Well, they're not very nice as a rule. Full of drunks and bad language. So I'm told," April added hastily. "Did you remain in your own chamber then on Wednesday evening?"

"I did. Reading one of Mrs. Radcliffe's novels, which was much more satisfying than, as you say, drunks and bad language."

April was delighted. "Oh, I like those. Which one are you reading?"

After a few pleasurable minutes of exchanging views of the scariest parts, April pulled the conversation back in line.

"Do you think you might have heard Stewart—that's his lordship's valet—and his friend come upstairs?"

Miss Camden considered. "I did hear voices speaking very quietly and then a door closed. It sounded like the one at the near end of the passage, though I suppose it might have been Darius's. I'm afraid I didn't look."

"Where is your room?"

"The third on the right-hand side. Darius is next to me, and Captain Lyall nearest the stairs. Mr. Murray has the room opposite."

"Did you hear Stewart come away again?"

"Someone passed in the passage, going toward the stairs."

"Did anyone walk past your door? That you noticed?"

"I heard Captain Lyall. His...walk is quite distinctive. He walked up and down the passage twice. I think he was exercising his bad leg."

"When was that?"

"Oh dear, maybe ten of the clock? Darius had come up ten minutes or so before. I definitely heard *his* door—"

April pounced. "Did he unlock it?"

Miss Camden opened her mouth, then closed it again and leamed back. "He says he did so, though to be honest I don't remember. It was certainly locked the next morning when he started roaring—I mean informing the house—of his loss. I rattled his door to find out what the problem was, and he had to unlock it to let me in."

"Hmm..."

Miss Camden inhaled. "I will be honest, Lady Petteril. My brother is forgetful. I am not certain that the purse was exactly where he said it was, on the table in his room. But I do know that we could not find it anywhere among his things or mine. Mrs. Barnes and the servants searched the taproom and the coffee room and could not find it there either. But unless it is found in the possession of Lord Petteril's valet, I really cannot see any evidence against him. Or anyone else."

"Was there much money in it?" April asked, since no one had yet mentioned the sum to her.

"A few guineas in coins, perhaps fifty pounds or so in bank notes. Not a ruinous amount, but considerable enough to be missed."

"And a great deal of money to some," April said. To servants, for example. "Do you have your own servants with you at the inn?"

Miss Camden shook her head emphatically. "I don't even *have* a lady's maid anymore. Travelling is less stressful without one, don't you find?"

"Oh yes," said April.

"So we just have our coachman. He sleeps above the stables with the inn's ostlers. I don't think the other guests have any servants. You are going to a lot of trouble for your husband's valet. He must be a very old retainer to be so valued."

Caught off guard by this sudden change of tack, April replied, "A few months." Then, as Miss Camden's brows rose, she added quickly, "But yes, we do value him. He did my husband a great service and we trust him implicitly."

SIR DARIUS CAMDEN DID not appear to be a tidy man.

Large and red-nosed, and probably fifteen or so years older than his sister, he sat scowling in his night gown, propped up in bed by many pillows. An array of leaves, mere stalks, and flowers were spread out on the coverlet, and a reference book lay open in his lap.

His room was cluttered. Cast off clothes lay on the floor and half out of drawers. A sleeve hung over the edge of an open trunk, almost as if someone had collapsed inside it. Notebooks and papers were piled on a chest of drawers among brushes and sleeve buttons.

Piers sat in the chair that had been set at some distance from the bed. Sir Darius clutched a huge handkerchief to his nose and sneezed mightily.

Piers gazed at him sympathetically. "It really is very good of you to see me in such circumstances."

"Oh, not at all," Sir Darius said. "Very grateful to you for taking an interest. The magistrate fellow didn't seem to know what he was about."

"Well, it's normally rather quiet here," Petteril said. Apart from the murder and mayhem of his last stay at Haybury. "Mr. Lindon is not much used to crime beyond drunken punch-ups."

"Not very used to it myself. It's not so much the money, Petteril, or even the inconvenience. It is *mine*."

"It is," Petteril allowed. "I have found in such affairs that it pays to be methodical, to establish all the facts in order to find the true perpetrator."

"Well, if you're convinced of your man's innocence, that's good enough for me." Sir Darius flapped one disparaging hand. "But it's not in *this* mess, for we looked yesterday. Tidied everything up and looked through every garment. I didn't mislay the purse or drop it."

"Tell me when you last saw the purse. I mean actually took note of it, not just assuming it was where you would normally have put it."

Sir Darius frowned. "I keep it in my coat pocket when I'm traveling. We stopped at an inn on the other side of Blanchester on Wednesday, about noon. I paid for a light luncheon and wine, so I definitely saw it then."

"Did you lay it down anywhere at this inn?"

To give him his due, Sir Darius thought about it. "No," he said triumphantly. "I paid and put it straight back in my pocket. In fact, I recall taking it out of my pocket here, in this room, later that afternoon. I put it *there*, on the table where the books are now, when I changed my coat."

"Did you go out after that?"

"Went for a stroll, just to stretch the legs, you know. And yes, I did lock the door. But I think I was already sickening, for we came back and had an early dinner."

"Did you go up to your room when you came back?"

Sir Darius began to look harassed, "Damn it, I don't know! I—no, I didn't. Kate did. M'sister. At least, she went to her *own* room to leave off her cloak and hat. I waited in the coffee room with a very nice glass of brandy."

"So when did you next go up to your room?"

"After we'd eaten. Escorted Kate back up to her room. I could feel this damned cold coming on and thought I should have an early night. Only then I decided another brandy would do me good, so I went down to the taproom where it was quite jolly."

"Did you go into your room before you went back down?"

"Yes, but not for very long. You're going to ask me if the purse was there, aren't you? And if the door was still locked."

"I am," Piers agreed.

"My feeling is, that it was there. That I'd have noticed if it wasn't. Hadn't had time to untidy the place, though I can't recall actually *looking*. But yes, I did lock the door."

"You remember *actually* doing that on *that* occasion?"

"Dash it, man, I always lock doors in these places when I can. Otherwise, I wouldn't leave my damned purse lying around."

Piers felt that point had gone as far as it could. "Then you unlocked the door when you returned?"

Sir Darius scowled blackly. "I did!"

"And the purse?"

"Didn't notice it one way or the other. Not until I woke up the following morning and saw it was gone."

Which, frustratingly, brought Piers no further forward. Sir Darius blew his nose and tugged at the skin of his neck as though to relieve a sore throat.

"What brought you here to the Red Lion, sir?" Piers asked.

Camden flapped his hand at the array of samples on the bed. "*Epipogium aphyllum.*"

Piers scratched around in the little used crevices of his brain. "The ghost orchid. It doesn't grow in England, does it?"

Camden's wan face lit up with delight. "You are a botanist, sir?"

"Sadly not. A friend of mine at Oxford was an enthusiast. He had heard rumours of the orchid growing in certain woods in this country, but he could find no record of it."

"I heard more than a rumour. I heard that it had definitely been sighted only weeks ago in woods around here. So I came looking. Actually, would you mind if I poked around in the Haybury wood?"

"Be my guest. I've found some unusual things there myself. Call and let me know how you get on. Bring your sister."

"I will. Very civil of your lordship."

"Not at all. By chance, are you acquainted with your fellow guest here, Mr. Murray?"

"We have met," Camden said without much interest. He was frowning at the flower on the end of a stalk that he held between his fingers. "Can't pretend it's anything like an orchid."

"No indeed. Which room is Mr. Murray's?"

Camden jerked his head. "Across the passage. Almost directly opposite."

"Thank you for your help," Piers said. "And I wish you a speedy recovery."

"Thank you, my lord, most amiable. Very glad to have met you. I'll let you know about the orchid. And the purse, if it turns up!"

Piers left, feeling as if he had just been banging his head against a wall to no purpose. He hoped April was faring better with the sister, and perhaps with the hotel servants.

Chapter Six

When Miss Camden retreated upstairs to breakfast with her brother, and Lord Petteril did not reappear, April wandered over to the taproom door and opened it.

Considering the early hour, she wasn't entirely surprised to find it empty. Even with the windows open, the smell hit her first—stale tobacco and ale—taking her back to her old life so fast that it made her queasy. How often had she entered places like this, offering to sweep up for a crust of bread? Somehow, she could never quite believe that old life was over. Even though here she stood, Viscountess Petteril.

And now that she actually looked, this place was nothing like the Silver Jug or the Queen's Head. The windows were open. There was no sawdust on the floor or unspeakable filth in the corners. No stray dogs slinking up with their poor tails between their legs, desperate for food but settling for a scratch behind their ears when she had none to give.

Leaving the door open, she sat on one seat after another, to discover whether or not she could see the stairs leading up from the coffee room. Mostly, she could.

There was a counter at one end of the taproom, behind which she found some stairs leading down to the cellar. Another door led out to the courtyard. She was just going to see if it was locked, when a maidservant bustled in, an empty laundry basket resting on her hip.

She was young, perhaps April's own age—whatever that was—and pretty, even with the unflattering mob cap she wore over her escaping light brown hair. She hadn't been at the Red Lion when April had last been here.

Catching sight of April, she squeaked. "Lawks, miss, what a fright you gave me! You don't want to be here in the taproom. Come through to the coffee room and tell me how I can serve you."

"It is more comfortable in there," April agreed, walking beside her in that direction. "Are you Verity?"

Her eyes widened with suspicion and something very like fright. "Yes, I am. Why?"

"I am Lady Petteril." Even saying the words gave her a little thrill of mingled pride and unease.

Verity dropped her basket and bobbed a frantic curtsey. "Sorry, my lady. I thought you'd left already."

"Not yet. His lordship is trying to get to the bottom of Sir Darius's missing purse. If you see what I mean."

"Mr. Stewart didn't take it," the girl said at once. "He wouldn't and he couldn't have anyway."

"I know he didn't," April said mildly. "How do *you* know?"

"Because it's beneath him. He's a very respectable gentleman, Lord Petteril's valet. And how's he supposed to have got through Sir Darius's locked door?"

"How could anyone else?" April countered. "What do you think happened?"

"I think he lost it," the girl muttered. "He's forgetful *and* untidy." As though realizing she was gossiping about a patron, she flushed a dull red. "Begging your pardon, my lady."

"No need," April assured her. "And if you're right, and the purse is never found, then I'd very much like to prove that Stewart could not have taken it. I believe you were in and out of the taproom, back and forth from the kitchen for most of the evening? Do you remember Stewart being there?"

"Yes, my lady. With Mr. Murray."

April lowered her voice conspiratorially. "Were they foxed?"

"Not much."

"Really? But Stewart had to help Mr. Murray up to his room."

Verity shrugged. "I didn't see that."

"Did you see Stewart come back to the taproom?"

She hesitated infinitesimally. "Yes, I saw that. He took his hat and went off out the taproom door."

"Thank you, that's helpful," April murmured, not entirely truthfully. "How long have you worked here, Verity?"

"Couple of months now."

"I'd say from your accent you're not from these parts."

"No, my lady. From Wiltshire."

"Goodness, that's a long way to come!"

"Mrs. Barnes is my godmother. She offered me the job when her last maid got married."

"Ah, I see. Do you like it here?"

"I do, my lady. Mr. and Mrs. Barnes are good to me and fair."

"Must be hard work though when the inn is busy."

"Oh, Tucker is here, too."

Tucker, April remembered. An amiable lad with a bit of reputation with the local girls. "Is he easy to work with?" she asked.

"Oh yes. He wouldn't try anything with me. Not now."

"I suppose not, your being Mrs. Barnes's goddaughter. Tell me, when you were busy on Tuesday evening, did any of the guests require anything upstairs?"

"No, my lady. Most of them were down here, except Miss Camden and she's such a considerate lady."

"What about Wednesday morning?" April asked. "Before Sir Darius discovered his purse was missing. Were you upstairs for any reason? Cleaning?"

"No, my lady. All the rooms were taken, so I waited till they were up and about."

"No early morning tea?" April asked with fading hope. "I was hoping you might have seen someone who perhaps shouldn't have been there. Or any guests moving about early."

"I didn't go up, my lady," she said woodenly. "I was helping Mrs. Barnes in the kitchen, preparing for breakfast."

"Of course you were," April sighed. "We're not having much luck, are we?"

It seemed to be the right thing to say, reminding the girl that they both believed in Stewart's innocence and, presumably, that no one was pointing a finger at Verity herself.

Yet.

PIERS WAS LUCKY ENOUGH to catch Mr. Neil Murray in his bed-chamber, about to go downstairs for breakfast.

"Yes?" came his response to Piers's knock.

Taking that as permission, Piers lifted the latch—no lock was employed here—and went in.

Mr. Murray had a larger room than Sir Darius, and it was spotlessly tidy, apart from the large bag, packed and open, sitting on the unmade bed.

"Mr. Murray?" Piers said amiably.

"Yes?" Murray said, blinking rapidly in surprise.

He looked to be in his mid-thirties, a few years older than Stewart, and less good-looking, with side-whiskers and a shiny face that somehow made him look greasy. However, no one knew better than Piers not to judge by appearances.

A frown pulled down Murray's brow. He was not happy to be bearded in his own chamber at this time of the morning. Piers did not blame him for that either.

"Forgive the intrusion," he said. "My name is Petteril."

Murray's eyes widened. "*Lord* Petteril? Stewart's master?"

"Exactly. I was hoping you could spare me a few words."

"Of course, my lord, of course! Let me begin by saying how sorry I am for what happened, especially as poor Stewart was in my company at the time. To all intents and purposes."

Piers lifted one eyebrow. "Then you saw him do it?"

Murray looked confused. "Do what? Take the purse? Of course I did not! I meant merely that we had been drinking in each other's company before it occurred. Will they let me see him before I go?"

Piers glanced at the packed bag. "Who? I will certainly let you if Stewart wishes it. You will find him at Haybury Court."

Murray's face was curiously expressionless. "They let him go?"

"There is no evidence against him," Piers said mildly. "The magistrate's investigation continues."

"You are a very forgiving master," Murray said slowly. "Most gentlemen would not be happy to take a man so tainted back into service."

"Tainted with what?" Piers asked.

"Theft, of course! The magistrate may not have solid evidence but he certainly found the grounds to arrest him."

"But not to charge him. You seem to know something I do not."

Murray's smile was secretive. "About Stewart, I know *many* things that you do not."

This kind of vague mud-slinging was always guaranteed to put Piers's back up. Thrown at Stewart, who had shown him loyalty and discretion well beyond his duties, it angered him.

He raised the larger quizzing glass to his eye and, very much the viscount, regarded Murray. "Are you going to elucidate?"

Murray gave another small smile, as though to say his lips were sealed under friendship.

"I thought not," the viscount drawled. "In which case, let us concentrate on Tuesday evening. Did you welcome Stewart's support up to your chamber?"

"I accepted it in the spirit in which it was given," Murray said evenly. "Which was friendship."

"Then you had not quarrelled?"

"Of course not," Murray scoffed. "If Stewart says so, he is lying."

Stewart, Piers suspected, was certainly lying about something, but at the moment, he found Murray's opinion more interesting. So he merely waited in silence and sure enough, Murray rushed into speech.

"It wouldn't be the first time, you know. You would not be throwing accusations at me if you truly knew his past!"

Piers allowed his lip to curl. He dropped the quizzing glass, which fell softly back to his chest. "I was not aware of having accused you of anything, Mr. Murray. Nor, for what it is worth, has Stewart. What time did you wake on Wednesday morning?"

"When Sir Darius Camden started shouting the odds."

"I see. I suppose you slept all night from the moment Stewart left you in your bed?"

"I did, my lord."

"Did he stay long to be sure you were—ah... comfortable?"

"He may perform such services for *you*, my lord. I was dumped unceremoniously and abandoned within seconds."

"How many seconds?" Piers inquired. "Ten? Or ten minutes' worth, which must be six hundred?"

"Sixty seconds," Murray said steadily. "One hundred at most. I already told the magistrate this."

"Ah yes, the magistrate," Piers said. "Since you seem about to depart, you should probably call upon him to leave your forwarding address. Or he may prefer you to stay until his investigation is concluded."

"In which case, I could support my friend Stewart," Murray said, although behind his suddenly caring expression, his eyes looked furious.

"You could," Piers agreed. He smiled beatifically. "Thank you for your help, Mr. Murray. Good morning."

Leaving the shiny man, he went back downstairs in search of April. It was probably past time to return to Haybury Court. Though with luck, they would have missed Aunt Hortensia altogether.

April was standing in the coffee room near the foot of the stairs talking to a maid servant, who shot off like a released arrow as soon as April lifted her gaze to Piers. There were pleasures and there were pains in being married to April.

"Shall we go?" he said, seizing his hat from the bench and striding to open the door.

April flexed her fingers, as though itching to write what she had learned into her once ubiquitous notebook. She had decided in Portugal that carrying it around made her too like a secretary and she would only write in it when she was alone. She walked out in front of him, unconsciously graceful and clearly desperate to talk.

A young man was rolling a barrel toward the cellar door, though seeing them, he paused to let them pass. He tugged at his cap, grinning familiarly.

"Tucker," April murmured. "The tapster."

"Just the man," Piers said, advancing, "How are you, Tucker?"

The tapster, a twinkly eyed, good-looking young man of perhaps twenty, replied, "Very well, my lord. Getting married next month."

"Good Lord! My felicitations!"

"Thank you!" He grinned again, including April. "And to you, my lord."

Piers inclined his head. "What do you make of this business of the stolen purse?"

Tucker took off his hat and scratched his head. "Don't seem much like Mr. Stewart. Not surprised the magistrate let him go. Not that we see him here often, so don't really know the man."

"How long do you think he spent upstairs after he took Mr. Murray up?"

"About ten minutes, I'd say."

In fact, Tucker told much the same story as everyone else, which must have bored April, for she began to wander a few steps away to admire the pot of flowers by the porch.

"How bosky were Stewart and Mr. Murray?" Piers asked.

"Bosky enough. Or at least Mr. Murray seemed to be. Didn't have that much, if you ask me. "

"You think he was pretending?"

Tucker shrugged. "We get all sorts in the taproom," he said, virtuously disapproving.

"How is the new maid doing?" April asked over her shoulder from the flowerpot.

"Verity? Well enough. Willing worker, though she don't say much."

"Pretty girl," April observed.

Tucker grinned. "I'm about to be married, my lady. I don't notice such things anymore. Besides, she's a bit of a dark horse, our Verity."

"In what way?" Piers asked, happy to follow April's line of questioning.

"Not my business," Tucker said hastily, and Piers realized he'd have to get him alone. Or ask Barnes.

April straightened. "I'll just step around to the stables and—"

A sudden, deafening crack rent the air and Piers's hat flew off his head. Before he even acknowledged it was a gunshot, he threw himself toward April.

But someone else catapulted into him. "Inside, my lord! Inside!"

Someone was tugging him toward the front door of the inn. A shiny man. Weasel-like features he had only just left. Neil Murray.

Piers brushed him off, able to think again now that his body shielded April's. "Don't panic. A random and very poor shot. Someone shooting a rat, probably. And even if not, it will take some time to reload."

Realizing he still had his arm around April's shoulders, he released her. Her eyes were wide and frightened for him, but still she pulled away, and went to pick up his hat. Piers moved with her, his eyes scanning the surroundings.

A random shot? Landing in the heart of the village. The green and the square itself appeared to be deserted, though a couple of women were scrubbing doorsteps.

April prodded the two holes in his hat with one trembling finger, then hastily reached up and plonked it on his head. Realizing what she was about, he moved back to where he was before as exactly as he could recall and reached up to find the hole. He swivelled.

"From the side of the church," he said thoughtfully.

Tucker took off at a run. "Let me get my hands on the stupid..."

"He'll be gone," Piers said. "Or at least hidden."

By this time, Barnes had appeared asking what the devil had made the noise, and Sir Darius was leaning out of his window in his nightgown, scowling ferociously.

"Home, I think," Piers murmured.

"Maybe we should take a carriage?" April said shakily. "What if he's still out there?"

"It doesn't make sense," Piers said, moving around the building to the stable yard. "Why would anyone shoot *me*?"

"'Cause the rent's too high? 'Cause they don't like lords? 'Cause they got a grudge? 'Cause..."

"Your accent's slipping," he said mildly. "I get the point. I am fit to be shot for any number of reasons, but why here and now?"

"Because you're asking questions about the theft," April said, her voice small and hard, a sure sign that she was frightened.

"He missed me," Piers said mildly.

"By an inch!"

"Oh, three, I'd say."

She cast him a look of dislike, almost snatching the mare's reins from the waiting ostler. "Thank you," she muttered.

Piers boosted her into the saddle before idly patting the Professor's nose. The horse nuzzled him, clearly glad to have him back. He mounted and tossed a coin to the grinning ostler.

April didn't speak as they made their way through the sleepy village.

Tucker, running back to the inn, stopped to give an eloquent shrug. "Couldn't see him. Probably after rats right enough. Better poisoning 'em than scaring the wits out of people. Think you'll need a new hat, my lord!"

"Cheaper than a new head," Piers said, and Tucker laughed.

April scowled her way ahead.

"Lady Petteril," Piers said mildly.

She straightened, smoothing her brow, but she was still rigid with tension. She remained silent until they were clear of the village.

Then, "Shooting rats?" she burst out. "At head height?"

"They run along gutters," Piers said.

"Damn it, why aren't you more...*worried*! The shot could have killed you!"

"It didn't," he pointed out. She was right though. He wasn't really worried. His brain was too busy replaying the scene and accurately placing everyone who had been present, including anyone in the square, particularly in the direction of the church...

On the other hand, April's genuine fear did touch him. It wasn't even for herself; it was for him. He remembered the time he was shot in the Queen's Head and the feel of her lips on his whispering in anguish, "*Don't die, don't die...*" He remembered that too often.

And finally, he recognized the true fear beyond her anger. She thought he didn't care if he died.

He reached across and closed his hand over both of hers on the reins. "April. I do care."

Her gaze flew up to his face, searching.

He withdrew his hand. She always wore gloves now, as a lady should. Sometimes, it didn't feel like an improvement. "I was just thinking. About the shot."

"There must be more to the theft," April said. "You don't shoot a lord just for being annoying."

He eyed her, and with relief caught her gleam of mischief. "I should indeed be riddled with bullets if that were the case," he acknowledged. "So, if it is to do with the theft, who could have done it? Not Tucker, Barnes, Murray, or Camden."

"Captain Lyall seems likeliest," she said with regret. "Pity, because I liked him."

"He is certainly used to firearms and being in the Rifle Brigade, he's probably an excellent shot. Hampered, though, by the lack of one arm."

"I'm sure he can still load and fire, would just take him longer. Especially if he had it loaded and ready. Would a pistol shot have reached you from the church?"

"A decent one, yes, I think so. But what the devil would he get out of it? What did I say that could have frightened him? Even if he stole the purse, he must know I can't prove it."

"Maybe someone else saw him. Or heard him. Miss Camden recognizes his footfall. She heard him go to his room that night and pace up and down the passage twice. She reckons he was exercising his bad leg, but he could have been watching or listening, waiting for Sir Darius to fall asleep. Miss Camden wouldn't necessarily have heard him going to her brother's later on."

"Officers and gentlemen have been known to steal," Petteril said. "But why would he? He's on his way home. Can't he pay his shot?"

"He doesn't want to go home," April said. "He feels useless, and I suspect he hates the pity constantly coming his way. From his family, he'll find it intolerable."

"Not sure fifty pounds would solve many of those problems."

"It's a start and he could make a career out of it."

"Unlikely, perhaps," Piers said.

"Well, it's either him or Miss Camden or Verity the maid. I'll wager anything you like that Miss Camden has learned to shoot somewhere along her adventurous life. Trouble is, I like her too."

"And the maid? Tucker was being a trifle...ambivalent about her."

"She has secrets," April allowed. She thought. "She could have dashed out the back door and gone the long way around to the church."

"Fetching a pistol on the way," Piers added.

"Hmm. It's still possible. Who else, then? Mr. Lindon, annoyed with you for springing Stewart and defending him? Unless the thief is someone entirely unknown to us, no one else is involved in the case. Apart from Stewart himself, of course."

Piers didn't answer.

She stared at him. "Seriously? You can't believe Stewart took that purse, then tried to kill you! Not you. He risked his life to *save* you."

"And you," Piers pointed out. "No. I can't see Stewart shooting me and I don't believe he took the money either. Not the Stewart we know. But what if there is a different Stewart?"

A frown tugged down her brow. "Stewart," she repeated, not in ridicule, but as though trying on the idea. "You mean, like I'm a thief?"

"Like you were," he corrected. "It doesn't stop you from being a good person."

"Am I?" she asked, apparently surprised, then, almost immediately, "You think Stewart used to be a thief? And still is, underneath?"

"Not sure we'd have much silver left if that was the case. But what if Stewart is not quite who and what we think he is? He took his incarceration very well, considering, almost as though he wasn't surprised. And when he came to the rescue at the Queen's Head, he was dashed handy with his fives. As they say."

"It wasn't his first fight," April said slowly. "Not respectable behaviour for a gentleman's gentleman. How did you find him in the first place?"

"The solicitor, Mr. Pepper, found him as he found the Parks and Benson." He frowned. "Or did Park find him? I can't remember."

"Did he have references?"

"Must have, or neither Pepper nor Park would never have sent him to me. He wasn't the first applicant I saw, but he was the first one I could bear. If I was shown his references, I didn't pay much attention." At that time, he hadn't been paying much attention to anything. He had been feeling his way out of profound blackness of spirit by means of acting, a stolen necklace, and a small thief called Ape.

"You should write to Mr. Pepper," April said.

"No need. He's coming down tomorrow."

"Why?" she asked in surprise.

"To draw up wills and settlements." He squared his shoulders. "Responsibilities of a married man, you understand."

Chapter Seven

Returning to the inn from her morning walk, Miss Kate Camden was not displeased to see a familiar figure limping in front of her, across the meadow that led from the wood to the back door of the inn.

Leaning heavily on his walking stick, Captain Lyall was making slow progress. But at least he stopped often, admiring the views or the clouds—or pretending to while he rested. She suspected he pushed himself too far.

She caught up with him quickly enough, for she was well used to exercise and as fit, according to Darius, as a flea.

"Well met, Captain," she said cheerfully. "It is a pleasant day is it not? The heat of summer has gone, but it is not yet quite autumn."

He looked round in surprise and bowed. "Miss Camden. Is it wise to walk alone?"

"No idea, but I often do. Darius usually accompanies me, but he is still prostrated by his cold."

To her surprise, a smile tugged at his lips, relaxing his rather hard face. "I would offer to walk in his place, but I am not much protection."

"Between you and me, I am not expecting much danger," she said with a confiding air, and this time, his eyes smiled, too. "It is pretty here, is it not? Do you have much further to journey? To your home, I mean."

The smile faded, leaving his face bleak and wintry. "Just the other side of the county. I could do it in a couple of days, probably, without changing horses. Why, are you going to offer me a seat in your carriage?"

"Oh, no," she said, "Darius would hate not being able to spread out his legs, and then we would all be miserable. You are much better riding alone."

"It was a joke," he muttered. "I would never be presumptuous enough to suggest such a thing if I meant it."

"No, you wouldn't," she agreed, "but it was not a joke, was it? You meant to deride yourself for frailty and me for pity. Take heart, Captain: I don't pity you. Or at least not beyond the occasional sympathetic *Ouch* when your leg clearly pains you."

"Good," he said uncertainly. Then, abruptly, he halted and added, "I'm being churlish. Sorry. I don't seem able to stop it."

"Oh, my brother has lots of days like that. Even I have a few and I, you must know, am very close to perfect. Tell me, what did you think of Lord and Lady Petteril?"

"I think they are eccentric and beguiling, and sharp enough to cut themselves and anyone else who steps too close."

Kate blinked at him curiously. "That's a very odd thing to say."

"You don't agree?"

"I don't know. There is something very appealing about him. And I rather liked her."

"That comes under the *beguiling* heading."

"And the sharpness?"

"It will get Sir Darius his purse back and probably some poor devil the noose."

"Better the guilty party than an innocent man." She frowned. "Or do you *know* who's guilty?"

Captain Lyall leaned on his stick and moved forward toward the inn's back gate without replying.

They found the inn in uproar. Darius's voice could be heard apparently, holding court from his bed, through the open door of his room, demanding to know how a gentleman, a peer of the realm, had been so nearly killed, even in the company of his lady wife.

"Is this a respectable inn?" he roared. "Is it a law-abiding community? Let's have that Lindon fellow back to sort out this nest of crime!"

"Who was nearly killed?" Kate demanded, hurrying up the stairs.

Everyone turned to her with that gleam of pleasurable outrage she had seen all too often before. Barnes was there, as was Mrs. Barnes, the maid Verity, Mr. Murray, and even Tucker the tapster. Inevitably, they all started talking at once.

Until Captain Lyall's walking stick cracked sharply against the banister, cutting through the swell of noise like a gunshot.

The silence was instantaneous.

"One at a time, if you please," Lyall said mildly.

He must have been a good officer, Kate thought irrelevantly, keeping his men in order without the aspect of bullying one saw so often. Even the bitterness had temporarily gone from his face, leaving it frankly curious, waiting for the intelligence of his troops.

"Barnes?" Lyall said.

"There was a gunshot, sir," the innkeeper said. "Scared us all out of our wits. Shot the hat right off Lord Petteril's head."

"Saw it with my own eyes," Tucker corroborated. "And when her ladyship picked it up, you could see clear as day, two holes where the ball passed through it. Must have missed his head by a hair's breadth."

"But that's terrible!" Kate exclaimed. "Who on earth would shoot his lordship?"

"Only a lunatic and a complete stranger," Mrs. Barnes said fiercely. "Everyone in these parts has known him since he were a sweet lad and wouldn't harm a hair on his head."

"Tell you what," Darius pronounced. "Probably the same misbegotten rogue who stole my purse. A crime spree, that's what it is. Kate, I won't have you here in such circumstances. Best pack your trunk."

"Oh, not today," Kate said, bustling into his room, and casting a quick smile at her brother's court before she closed the door on them. "I don't think you should risk traveling just yet and besides—what about *epipogium aphyllum?"*

A wistful look crossed his watery eyes, and she pressed home the advantage without examining her motives too closely.

"We haven't even been out looking for it yet, not properly."

"That is true, but dash it, Kate, can't have you associating with a parcel of thieves and murderers!"

"I thought we were agreed it was the same person?" Kate said. "And a stranger at that. I promise I shan't go out walking alone anymore, and by the time you are up to going out, I'm sure the fellow will be caught."

He took longer to be persuaded than she had expected—he really was a kind brother and took her safety seriously—but by the time she left him with his book and a couple of clean handkerchiefs, he had agreed they should stay at the inn at least a couple of days longer.

As she closed her own bedchamber door, she glimpsed a figure further along the passage. She wondered if it was Captain Lyall and felt a warm glow of excitement. She didn't know why she liked him, but she did. The knowledge should have set off warning bells in her mind, but it didn't. It pleased her.

Abandoning her pelisse and bonnet, she picked up her novel and went down to the coffee room to read it and see if she couldn't learn more of the odd shooting of Lord Petteril. Drawn to the more interesting and eccentric of people, she had liked the couple, though in truth she knew very little about them.

The coffee room was not empty. Mr. Murray sat at the table nearest the front door, a map spread out on the table before him. Kate hesitated. Her instinct was to bolt back to her room, but pride would not let her give in to fear. She nodded distantly to him and went to sit at the corner table. She asked the bustling Verity for a cup of tea which was brought to her very quickly.

She had just settled into her book when Mr. Murray's shadow fell over her.

"Miss Camden." He bowed and, without invitation or permission, pulled up a chair and sat down, just a little too close.

"Mr. Murray," she said frigidly. "Is there something I can do for you?"

"Oh, I just came to drop a friendly word in your ear. I feel we are all comrades here at the inn, given all that has happened."

"Do you?"

"Madam, are you in the habit of frequenting the public rooms of hostelries without escort? I cannot think your brother would approve."

"Why don't you ask him?" Kate said pleasantly. She would put her fingers in her ears when he did.

Murray ignored that. "I hope you have not forgotten what we discussed before. That I am on quite excellent terms with the proprietors of several widely read newspapers."

"You mean scandal rags," she corrected with contempt.

He sat back, smiling. "You needn't be so high-and-mighty, Miss Camden. I well remember the scandal that filled those—er... rags, only a few years ago—yes, even as far as Scotland."

Dear God, was she never to have any peace from that? Even here, in this obscure corner of the country, in this quiet, rural inn? She thought she had shut this vile little man up, but apparently not.

"I know you don't want that all raked up again. It must have been so uncomfortable at the time."

Uncomfortable did not begin to cover it. She did not speak, but it seemed she didn't need to. Murray had the floor.

"We have already established that you wouldn't like Mrs. Barnes to know, for example." He smiled. "Or Lady Petteril. Yet now you leave yourself open to fresh criticism that the newspapers would love to publish—skulking alone in a public inn while your brother is ill."

"I have already paid you," Kate said between her teeth. "Now leave me alone."

"And," Murray continued as if she had not spoken, "immediately after he has been the victim of theft. What would the—er... *scandal rags* make of that?"

BY THE TIME SHE REACHED Haybury Court, April had recovered from her fright, if not from her anxiety. For most of the journey, her heart had felt as if it was in her mouth, choking her with the horror of what had so nearly happened.

Lord Petteril could be dead. Piers. Her husband.

His life snuffed out. And hers, to all intents and purposes.

But at least it was the thinker in him who seemed to have taken over, not the melancholic. She was not *that* unbearable as a wife. *"I care,"* he had said. About life and about her. He was still her friend.

All the same, while her head buzzed with possibilities about the shooting and the theft and the people surrounding both events, she felt she was grappling with something larger, something much more personal.

When they trotted up to the head of the gravel drive, a travelling carriage and horses were already standing at the front door. For once, remembering the company, April waited for Petteril to lift her down. Then she patted Lady's neck and gave the mare's reins to Jem the stable lad who had run over from the carriage. He led both horses away, and Petteril drew April's hand into the crook of his arm as they walked around the carriage.

The dowager viscountess and Gussie stood at the front step, supervising the bestowal of their baggage. Or at least, the dowager did.

"Piers!" Gussie hurried toward them before her mother could stop her. "I'm so glad we caught you, even if only to say goodbye. When are you coming to London next?"

"I'll let you know," Petteril said, submitting to Gussie's enthusiastic hug. He even patted her back.

Affection pleased him, April realized, stupidly surprised. There had been, perhaps, too little in his life.

Gussie didn't try to embrace April—much to April's relief—but she did surprise her by taking her hand.

"Look after each other," she said, her sparkling eyes including them both.

Petteril bowed to his aunt. "Safe journey, Aunt Hortensia. Gussie."

Aunt Hortensia sniffed. "Goodbye, Piers."

He handed her into the carriage, and Gussie after her, then raised the step, closed the door and stood back beside April, who raised her hand to Gussie, at least, with friendly intent.

"Something has put her out," Petteril observed.

"You made a bad marriage."

"No, it's more than that. I was too annoyed with her before to register it, but she's *very* miffed. It can't just be shame at our marriage. She had already washed her hands of me and told all her friends I would destroy the viscountcy. She's more than contemptuous. She's furious."

"Maybe she holds you in more affection than you thought."

Petteril thought about it. "Nah," he said and walked up the steps to the house.

"Your accent slipped," April said provokingly as she followed him. "Or was it your diction?"

"Both, I expect." He bowed her into the house with a flourish. "Breakfast, my lady?"

Breakfast alone with Lord Petteril was just what she needed. He dismissed the servants after they brought fresh tea and coffee and eggs to supplement the array of food already out on the sideboard. April, helping herself, breathed a sigh of relief. This was like Portugal again. Just the two of them, and no one to judge. Not in this room anyhow.

Unfortunately, it could not last, for he went off to teach his reading class in the library to those of the household who wished to learn, and then he had estate matters to see to with his steward, Sullivan Daniels.

And she had to meet with Mrs. Hicks later to discuss the running of the house, a prospect that filled April with awkwardness and a sense of helplessness. To distract herself, she went up to her own sitting room and took out her new notebook, where she wrote down everything she had learned about the theft and the people at the inn. Then she added her own speculations.

She still could not write fast enough to keep up with her brain, but as she read over what she had written, she could not help being pleased with the neatness of her letters, although she suspected her spelling was...idiosyncratic. She practised every day and his lordship was a good teacher.

His lordship. Panic surged into her stomach as she remembered how close she had come to losing him. Forcing herself, she wrote that down too, including the direction of the shot and who could possibly have fired it.

She was concentrating so hard on what she had observed just before the shot that she didn't hear the housekeeper enter the room.

"It *is* you!" Mrs. Hicks exclaimed from several feet away.

April stopped writing, dragging her mind back to the present. She glanced over her shoulder with a quick smile. "I wondered how long it would take you."

Mrs. Hicks grasped the back of a chair as though to prevent herself collapsing into it. "Blow me down!"

"Sit, Mrs. Hicks," April said kindly. She replaced her pen in the stand and shoved the still open book into her desk drawer before she rose.

The housekeeper was sitting in one of the comfortable chairs, the book and papers she carried fallen into her lap. She still looked stunned.

"It's not a secret," April said.

"But your voice, your speech, the hair...clothes..."

"He is the viscount," April said by way of explanation.

"And now you're the viscountess." There was definite hostility creeping into the housekeeper's voice. "Which is the real you?"

April sat down in the chair next to Mrs. Hicks. "Both."

"Stupid, so stupid." Mrs. Hicks shook her head, whether at herself or April wasn't clear. "I even thought you were like her. I wasn't even surprised, to be honest, because I always thought..." She trailed off, colouring, and straightened her back. "It was just when I saw you writing, there, in that book of yours that I realized. You must be having a proper laugh at us."

"Of course I'm not," April said indignantly. "To tell the truth, I was slightly hurt none of you knew me. And I never expected it to be easy, coming back here as his wife. You don't need to tell me I'm not worthy of him. I always knew that. But this is what he wants, and I won't have him annoyed by...complaints, spoken or otherwise."

"We heard a rumour you were some heiress his lordship met abroad."

"That was the dowager Lady Petteril's doing, to hide the truth which naturally appals her."

Mrs. Hicks nodded as though that made sense. "He always went his own way, Mr. Piers..." Her expression softened for a moment, then hardened again. "Is that why you went abroad? To marry him?"

"No. We went abroad to find Major Withan who had gone missing. We found him and he was there when we married. I'm not going to discuss that." April looked her in the eye. "Do we have a problem, Mrs. Hicks? Do you feel yourself unable to work for me?"

Mrs. Hicks stared back. "Do you want me to go?"

"No, I want you to stay, and help me make himself comfortable."

A smile flitted across the housekeeper's plump face and vanished again. "I always thought you had a good heart, but God knows this isn't what I would have chosen for him."

"Nor I," April agreed. "The trouble is, his lordship does his own choosing."

"And you don't?" Mrs. Hicks said shrewdly.

"Of course I do. And I will always choose him."

It was more than she meant to say, and heat seeped into her cheeks. But for some reason, the words seemed to settle Mrs. Hicks, who took a deep breath, nodded once, and pushed the loose paper across the table to April.

"These are Mrs. Drake's proposed menus for the rest of this week. She is happy to discuss any changes you might want to make. I was proposing to show you the inventory of linen, china, glass, and silver before we discuss any changes you might want to make. But since you already know how the house is run..."

"I don't really," April said. "Only bits of it. You manage the whole house and I see no point in changing things that work perfectly well. If something bothers me, I'll discuss it with you. Shall we start with the linen?"

"Perfect," said Mrs. Hicks, lumbering to her feet.

AT THE RED LION, NEIL Murray sat in the taproom, staring morosely into his ale.

He was torn.

He really wanted to shake the dust of this place from his feet and bolt for London. He could take the stagecoach from Blanchester this evening. Only, if he did so without seeing the magistrate first, would that cast suspicion on him? Would he have time to lose himself in the anonymity of London? Should he risk going to the magistrate and asking?

On the other hand, he really needed to see Stewart again before he went. He almost regretted pointing Stewart's bumbling master at his valet's past. Not quite, for he did enjoy seeing the bastard squirm. Only he couldn't get at him with Stewart locked in the fastness of Haybury

Court. Was he even allowed to leave the house when it wasn't his day off? How could he live like that?

No, domestic service was not for Neil Murray.

Inns, however, were an excellent hunting ground. One met all sorts at inns, from baronets to pot-washers, all squashed under one roof without the same kind of segregation as one found outside the inn walls. Traveling people were temporarily rootless and much more liable to spill interesting information about strangers.

Which made them much easier to rob.

As Sir Darius Camden had recently discovered. And his sister.

The pretty maidservant breezed into the taproom, greeting the regular drinkers she passed on her way to the common room door. She carried a basket full of laundry which had presumably being drying in the sun. Beneath the basket, in her apron pocket, a corner of paper poked out.

Murray had not made a success of his life by ignoring opportunities, however unlikely they seemed.

He sprang to his feet. "Let me get that door for you."

"Thank you, sir."

Reaching past her, he opened the door with his right hand, while with his left, he twitched the paper from her apron and pocketed it.

He smiled at her. "May I buy you a glass of sherry when you are free?"

"Thank you, sir, but I'm always on duty. Not allowed to consort with the patrons." She smiled and nodded, all very cool and practised. A girl used to turning away the advances of drunks in her place of work. And yet she used words like *consort*. She had some education.

He inclined his head, contriving to look both disappointed and understanding. Which he was.

Closing the door behind her, he sat down again, took a sip of his ale and cast a quick glance at the regular drinkers, deep in conversation with young Tucker the tapster. Murray took his booty from his pocket and found a letter addressed to a woman in Wiltshire.

Breaking the seal without compunction, he unfolded it and read it with great interest. He began to smile.

AS ALWAYS, APRIL LOOKED forward to dinner with Lord Petteril. She had just donned her evening gown and was contorting herself to try and fasten the back, when she heard him enter her sitting room.

"April?" he called urgently.

At once, she straightened the dress so that it fell around her properly and hurried into the sitting room.

"It wasn't meant for me," he said.

"What wasn't?" she asked, bewildered.

"The shot. Think about it," he added, as she turned her back to show him the unfastened hooks. At once he came over to fasten them for her—an old ritual from Portugal days, and before, onboard the ship. "Murray was upon me instantly. He must have been skulking just outside the doorway, probably listening to our conversation with Tucker."

The memory swam before her eyes, the flowers in the pot, Tucker refusing to speak about the maid, Verity, and...

"There was a shadow," she said excitedly, beginning to spin around.

"Hold still," his lordship said severely.

"Sorry. But the shadow must have been Murray. It went out of my head because of the shot, but you could be right that the gunman was aiming at him. Which begs the question..." She broke off, distracted by the brush of his fingers against her nape as he wrestled with the fiddly top fastenings.

She dipped her head, her heart beating faster. She had also had her epiphany, when she had contemplated losing him. It had taken her most of the afternoon to understand it, but it had to do with the shortness of life, the suddenness of unalterable death, and the need to not merely exist but to *live*. And to love without fear.

His fingers stilled on her skin. She didn't know if the hook was fastened or not. Her breath quickening, she turned to face him.

His eyes were so dark they were often unreadable. Deliberately so. She thought something desperate passed through them now. His hands fell to his side, but he did not step back.

"Begs what question?"

April couldn't remember. "Murray," she said at random. Then, "Why would anyone shoot Murray? Why would Captain Lyall shoot Murray?"

"We don't know that it *was* Lyall, only who it was not."

He stepped back, which at least meant she could breathe again. And think.

The moment was small, but at least it had been there.

She swallowed. "Stewart might have reason to shoot Murray," she said, low. "But I don't believe he would risk you in order to do it."

"But if it wasn't aimed at me, the shot likely has nothing to do with the theft. Whatever Stewart's past, I'm fairly sure Murray's is considerably less savoury. Perhaps we should be enquiring about strangers in the area. Do you want a shawl?"

"No, thank you. The evening is warm enough." She took his arm. "If the shooter was a stranger with any sense, he'd already have bolted for Blanchester or wherever he came from."

"Probably."

Since they could not discuss Stewart and the theft in front of the servants, they talked about the estate, with which Petteril seemed pleased, and about April's introduction to the household treasures of china and silver.

After the meal, rather than linger on his own over the brandy, he picked up the decanter and accompanied her to the drawing room. The room had been refurbished in April's suggested colours, so she found it much more pleasant to be in. Opulent, of course, and very large. But she chose to sit beside him on the sofa so that conversation was easy, and she could enjoy the pleasure of his nearness.

"*I won't touch you,*" he had said in Portugal. "*I propose a marriage in name only.*"

It had been a beginning and she had been content to wait. Until he had almost been shot—again—and she understood there were fates neither of them could control. She also understood that any change in their marriage would have to come from her. And in this, she, who had seen more of life than he ever could, was woefully inexperienced.

So they sat together but not touching, each with a book open on their lap, reading by candlelight as the early autumn night drew in, occasionally talking of the theft and sometimes of things that had nothing to do with it.

Her stomach was full of butterflies as they doused the candles and made their way up to bed. As always, he lit her to her rooms, where a lamp was already burning low.

"Oh, could you help me with these hooks before you go?" she asked, barely able to get the words out for the hammering of her heart. "I'm afraid I'll tear the fabric, wrenching it around."

"Of course." He came in and set down his candle, turning up the lamp at the same time.

She turned her back and felt him come up behind her. She bent her head and shivered as his deft fingers unfastened her gown.

Stay. Please stay.

Over-aware of his every move, she knew when he reached the last hook, and turned quickly before he could move away.

"Thank you," she said, smiling, because she knew he liked her smile. Her heart pounding now, she reached up and kissed his cheek. She had only ever kissed him once before, on the lips when she had thought he was dead.

She drew back enough to look into his face, searching for lust or disgust, and found only warmth. He was...*touched*.

He took her hand and hope surged as he raised it to his lips.

"Good night, April."

Whatever she would have blurted in response to that was lost in wonder as he bent his head to hers and gently kissed her cheek.

And then he was gone, softly closing the door behind him.

She didn't know whether to throw something after him or laugh. Or cry.

She had no seductive arts. Most of her life had been spent repelling. She had seen the whores enticing customers, of course, but some instinct or good sense prevented her trying their wiles. There had only ever been honesty between her and Petteril.

Except by omission.

"Oh well," she said ruefully, walking towards the window. "Tomorrow is another day." And he would still be here. Her husband. If nobody shot him.

Restlessly, she sat down at her desk and took out the notebook again. She updated it with Petteril's theory of Murray being the true target. If that was true, then she was sure Stewart was not the culprit. Not that he was not capable of killing, she reflected—she remembered him in that fight at the Queen's Head—but not from a distance and not when he had so little chance of hitting his mark.

She wafted the quill feather over her nose a few times, deep in thought, then she put it back in its stand, sanded what she had written, and decided to read over all her notes to see if that inspired any more ideas.

It didn't. The words blurred before her eyes...

She woke with her cheek stuck to the book. Annoyed, she peeled her skin carefully away from the paper and peered at it for signs of smudging. One of the candles was guttering, so she got up to pinch it out.

Then a light from the window caught her eye.

A moving light, bobbing in the darkness like a lantern. Quickly, she doused most of the candles and turned down the lamp. It was almost midnight, so who would be out with a lantern?

She saw it again at once, approaching the folly. A lovers' tryst? Or was someone up to mischief? Like trying to shoot Lord Petteril again. Well, she wasn't having that.

Stepping out of the evening gown, she dropped a walking dress over her head instead and grabbed her old cloak. Then she picked up the remaining candle and left her rooms. There she hesitated.

Every instinct told her to wake Lord Petteril so they could investigate together. But that was madness if it was Petteril they'd come for. No, this was a strictly spying mission, and she would do better alone.

She ran lightly down the main staircase and around to the side door, where she collected a lantern and lit it from her candle. Covering the lantern with a shawl so that it shone only where she wished, she eased back the bolts and crept outside.

The whole house was in darkness as she hurried along the path to the folly, even the windows of the viscount's apartments. She hoped he was asleep, for he would probably be up again at dawn riding. He had devils, had Lord Petteril, and she suspected his morning rides in all weather was how he kept them at bay.

She approached the folly with caution, stepping off the path just before the ground rose. Here, she could hide behind the ancient oak tree and see who was at the folly. If they were still there. She tugged the shawl over the rest of the lantern just before she reached the tree.

The complete darkness baffled her for an instant, but she knew she only had to take two steps and she would feel the trunk of the tree. One—

An arm like steel closed around her waist, hauling her back against a hard body. At the same time, a hand clapped over her mouth. The lantern fell and went out, and black fear hit her like a fist.

Chapter Eight

Verity Small was exhausted after a long shift at the Red Lion. Mrs. Barnes had already gone to bed, and now that everything was ready for the morning in the kitchen and the common room, she could retire too. Mr. Barnes and Tucker would throw out the lingering drinkers.

Emerging from the kitchen, yawning and longing for bed, she was more annoyed than frightened when she saw the shadow moving in the semi-darkened common room.

It rose from a bench in the corner and glided toward her candle, causing her a twinge of unease until she recognized him.

"Oh, Mr. Murray. Is something wrong? The house is—"

"Well, yes, I would say there is something wrong. In such a respectable house."

"I'm very sorry to hear that, sir, though I can't imagine what you mean."

Murray smiled. In the glow of her candle, his oily features looked somehow sinister. She remembered the way he had looked at her in the taproom that afternoon and wondered whether she should call out for Tucker. He might hear her, even through the closed door to the taproom, though it might also wake the guests upstairs...

"You, my dear," Murray purred. "Apparently so young and innocent and virtuous, and yet..."

A jolt of fear passed through her. "Sir, you're a guest in this house, but you've got no call and no right to insult me."

"I haven't insulted you. I know the truth. You are a whore, are you not?"

Fury and shame swept over her. "How dare you?" She swung away from him, had already taken two strides toward the front door before he spoke again.

"A child out of wedlock," he said, and she had to grasp the edge of the table for support.

Blood sang in her ears.

"I don't know what you mean," she managed.

Something rustled behind her and she spun around to face her tormentor, who waved a letter at her, still smiling. Instinctively, she plunged her hand into her apron pocket.

Oh, dear God... She had been so busy, she had forgotten to put it with the rest of the post for collection. It must have fallen out of her pocket.

She tried for pride, when inside, she was cringing. "I hope you have not stooped to reading other people's private letters."

"So self-righteous," he mocked. "I have your secret. Now, do I tell the redoubtable Mrs. Barnes? Because I doubt *you* have."

The candle flame shook as she trembled. It was all falling apart again. Mrs. Barnes would dismiss her, goddaughter or not. Oh, she would be kind about it, understanding, even, but the result would be the same. No money to send to her sister for Hope's upbringing. Another hunt for work. She didn't even know if Mrs. Barnes would give her a character after this...

"Don't tell her," she blurted. "I will, later, in my own way."

He pretended to consider. "That would not suit me. I need to see more immediate results."

"Then stop talking in riddles," she snapped, "and tell me what you want."

Instead of angering him, her show of spirit seemed to delight him, for his teeth gleamed. "And a temper! How thrilling. I am something of a merchant, my dear. Money buys my silence."

She blinked. "But I have no money."

He waved the letter again. She wanted to snatch it but knew he could easily hold it out of her reach. Besides, dignity seemed to be all she had left.

"No money?" he repeated. "This letter says otherwise. It does sound like a pittance, your wage, but it all helps the righteous, does it not? Besides, you write you should have more this week, thanks to the generosity of wealthy patrons. I believe you are paid tomorrow. I am prepared to wait."

She stared at him. "But if I pay you, I have none for Hope."

"Then you should tell the truth and work harder, should you not?"

Any residual pride she might have had left, vanished into the night. "Sir, I beg of you. She is my child. Without my money..."

He flapped one hand to silence her. "Yes, yes. I suppose you may pay in kind."

"In kind?" she repeated, uncomprehending.

He smiled. "You would, of course, have to be very, very kind."

FOR YEARS, APRIL HAD reacted to any aggression, any touch, almost before it happened. With lightning reflexes, she could dodge, kick, elbow, and wriggle herself out of harm's way. But this attack was so sudden, so reminiscent of the memory she never thought of, that for an instant, it paralyzed her.

But only for an instant. She jerked her elbow forward—preparing to ram it back into her attacker—and wrenched open her mouth against the firm palm.

"Don't bite," her captor breathed in her ear. "It's me."

Him. His hand left her mouth, his arm loosened, and she flung herself around, gasping, and seized him around the neck, her fingers clutching convulsively as she inhaled his familiar smell. She should have known from his hand...

He laid his cheek on her hair, just for a moment, but it was enough.

"What?" she whispered. "Who's there?"

He drew her around the tree, from where she could see the folly. Something glowed faintly on the far side of it, mostly hidden, she suspected, from the house.

Together, Petteril and April edged around the folly mound. She could hear the faintest hum of voices. Two people, one male, one female, talking very quietly.

A lover's tryst, then. In her relief, she would have turned to go back, only Petteril's fingers curled around her hand, drawing her on around the foot of the folly. She was afraid of tripping in the darkness, or disturbing stones or dry twigs underfoot.

By the dim lantern light, a couple were outlined, sitting on the ground behind the building, their backs to April and Petteril. His lordship dropped into a crouch, tugging her with him. He fumbled for his quizzing glass and raised himself just enough to see over the mound.

He dropped back and pulled the quizzing glass ribbon over his head before passing it to April. Honoured, she took it and straightened.

The couple sat close together but did not touch like lovers. Even from the back, she thought she knew the man's shape and posture, but she raised the quizzing glass to her eye, almost shocked by the magnification.

The man turned his head toward the woman. Oh yes, it was Stewart.

He looked slightly sinister in the flare of the lantern. She had never imagined him in that way before. The woman wore a cloak, the hood over her hair and hiding any possible glimpse of her face. But April knew something of that stiff, wary posture, the faint, nervous twitch of her arm. She was frightened. But proud.

Was it Mavis the housemaid? She had always had a certain glint in her eye when she looked at Stewart.

They both stood and April dropped down again. She handed the glass back to Petteril, who edged upward again, then straightened altogether.

"They're taking the shortcut to the road," he murmured. He shifted position, peering more closely. "There's a horse down there. She must have ridden here."

Not Mavis, then. Or... "He's not legging it, is he?"

"Lady Petteril," he scolded without turning.

After a few moments of silence, she got up impatiently to see for herself. She could see the bobbing lantern light getting closer to the outline of the horse. Stewart lifted her into the saddle.

"Can you see her face?" April demanded, wondering if she should look instead.

"No," he said regretfully, "but she's going in the direction of the village."

"Someone from the inn?" Her breath caught. "Miss Camden!"

"Despite previous observations, it isn't exactly common for ladies to indulge in any kind of relationship with a servant."

"Did they look like lovers to you?" she retorted. "Stewart could be helping her with something."

"Like stealing from her brother?" Petteril asked dubiously. "I'm sure she has rather more than fifty pounds of her own to spend."

"Why, did you ask her? She's probably got nothing Sir Darius doesn't give her."

"Yes, but she seems fond of her brother."

April sighed. "True. But she's frightened of something, whoever she is."

He didn't dispute it. He trusted her on the subject of fear. "What would Miss Camden have to be afraid of? She's brave enough to junket about the country with her brother rather than stay at home with her needlework and go to balls and tea parties."

"What if he compels her?" April mused. "She put up an excellent display for me, but there's a restlessness in her that she's hiding. What if Sir Darius isn't the harmless if forgetful and irascible man we think he is? What if she's afraid of him?"

"What indeed?" he said thoughtfully. "Come on, let's get back to the house before Stewart beats us to it and locks us out."

April rediscovered her dropped lantern by feel, and Petteril took the flint and tinder box from his pocket to relight it.

They walked toward the house, each thinking their own thoughts. It seemed his were not all about Stewart and the theft either, for he said, "I'm sorry I startled you. I just didn't want you to give away our presence by accident."

"I ain't—I'm *not* that stupid," she muttered. She was still rattled, though. Otherwise she wouldn't have slipped back into her old speech. She hardly ever did that now.

"I didn't know why you were there," he said mildly.

"I was following the light. I saw it from my window and wondered if it was another threat to you."

"I'm pretty sure the threat is not to me."

She turned to him. "Why are you here? Did you see the light too?"

"No, I was here before Stewart. I fear he has usurped my favoured brooding spot. She arrived about five minutes later."

"An assignation," April mused. "But not a romantic one."

"Not overtly so," he agreed.

She thought a bit more, then frowned, reverting to his earlier words. "What were you brooding about?"

"You, mainly."

Her heart skipped a beat. She had expected some insight into the theft or Stewart's odd behaviour.

"M-me?" she said uncertainly. "Am I making too many mistakes?"

"Lord, no." The swinging lantern lit up the quirk of his lips. "From where I stand, you've made none. I have the feeling the entire household has realized who you are but none of them are letting on to the others. It's a kind of respect."

"For you," she said proudly.

"Mostly for you."

She felt warm with embarrassment and something else she couldn't recognize. "I never expected that."

"Truth be told, neither did I," Petteril admitted. "Though perhaps I should. You are a remarkable little creature."

It wasn't the kind of compliment many women would have valued, but it made April glow with pleasure and pride.

"Who did you think I was when I startled you?"

Like a bucket of cold water, that wiped the smile off her face. She opened her mouth to turn the question aside with aggression or jest, she scarcely knew which would blurt out.

Honesty. I insisted on honesty. We promised each other that.

She swallowed. "I've forgotten. I never think about it."

He took her hand. "Then we won't."

She gazed up at him in wonder. How could she ever want more than she had in this moment?

AT FIRST LIGHT, PIERS rode the Professor across the meadow, where he could give the horse his head and let him gallop to his heart's content. It did Piers good, also. He had too much to think about—and not to think about—to feel very *steady*, and the exercise helped clear his mind and tire his body.

Pepper, his solicitor was calling on him today, and he had hopes of learning more from him about Stewart's past. Or at least if there was anything he should look into. After that, he would need to speak to Stewart again, find a way to make the valet trust him.

April trusted him.

It was a hard-won trust and all the more valuable for that. It had become an almost sacred duty to maintain it. After all, he had plucked her from her unspeakable old life. He hadn't needed to plunge her into the different morass that was his own. Having done so for so many reasons—whatever hers were for agreeing—the responsibility was one he could never shirk.

It was getting harder, though. Sitting close beside her, every nerve aware that she was his wife. And if he didn't know better, he would have imagined she flirted with him last night. He blinked away the vision of her slender, bent neck, the curve of her smooth shoulders, the freckle just beneath her nape.

She had kissed him. Not through fear of his death, just from affection. A brief, chaste salute that still released a deluge of longings. And hope. Which somehow made everything else more difficult.

How had he ever imagined a celibate marriage to *her* would be easy?

Sometimes, now, in his dreams, she danced across the attic, through the dust that sparkled in shafts of sunlight, and straight into his arms.

He dug in his heels, urging the Professor to greater speed.

Undoubtedly it helped. By the time he walked the Professor past the folly, things were back to manageable proportions. He halted and dismounted, patting the horse's nose and neck before he ambled up the mound and around the folly.

He wasn't quite sure what he was looking for—some hint, perhaps, of who Stewart's companion had been.

He wished he had just walked up to them last night. Then he would at least have known if she was significant. But for some reason, he was loathe to invade the man's privacy so obviously. It seemed to have become a kind of code between them. Stewart never let him know he was aware of anything in his life, although he must have been. Even trying to protect him, Piers owed him the same dignity.

He poked about the stones of the fake ruin as he went, from the outer wall to his own favourite rock and around the back to the other side where Stewart and his mysterious companion had been sitting.

He could see the scuff marks of Stewart's shoes, the indent in the grass where they had sat, and behind that, close against one of the bricks, was a small, narrow gap. There was earth, soft earth, recently turned, but the grass and weeds did not grow so close to the stone as they did everywhere else.

Crouching down, he dug his fingers into the earth. It came easily, along with the grassy surface that had clearly been only pressed back on recently. He felt a bit like a dog digging up a bone with his paws, but he did eventually pull out his prize.

A brown leather purse.

SIR DARIUS CAMDEN DISCOVERED he felt well enough to dress and go downstairs to break his fast. Having dragged a comb through his hair—it made little improvement—he wondered if he felt up to walk to Haybury woods in search of the elusive ghost orchid.

Turning, he picked up his room key from the table with one hand, and reached for his purse with the other, before he recalled he no longer had the purse and scowled at the empty table. Still, the action felt like a habit. Did he not always do that? Even at home? Why had he not done it on Tuesday evening?

Or had he?

He paused, his hand on the latch. He had a memory of picking up the key and the purse from that table. But had it been when he went for a walk with Kate? Or when he went to the taproom?

It didn't really matter. Either way, the wretched purse had gone. Still, it made him uneasy that he couldn't recall. This was beyond eccentrically forgetful. It felt rather like a drunk's lost memory.

Shaking off the shame, he left the room and locked the door. He could hear Kate's voice drifting up from the common room. She sounded her old, lively self, which did his heart good. Until he reached the head of the stairs and saw her seated at a table with Captain Lyall.

Oh, don't Kate, not again...

Why could he not be glad for her? She had learned her lesson. She was no longer a giddy, trusting girl. But she still hadn't grasped that no gentleman, not even a broken one like Captain Lyall, would ever marry her.

The fault was his. Engrossed in his studies, he had failed to look after his little sister properly, and she had paid the price.

So he scowled furiously at Captain Lyall as he strode across the room and took his place beside Kate.

APRIL SAT DOWN TO BREAKFAST alone. She couldn't get over the array of food provided for two people. Seven months ago, a crust of bread, a scrap of too-old meat, had been a treasure. Now, her leftovers were parcelled up and given to the poorest families on the estate.

She wasn't sure how she felt about that. Everyone should eat. She just remembered that whenever she had a penny, it had given her pride to buy her own, rather than beg, borrow and steal someone's scraps.

One of her new duties, Petteril had told her, would be to visit the Haybury tenants and labourers, giving what advice and help she could. She, who knew nothing about country living. She should talk to his lordship about that, and Mr. Daniels the steward. And Mrs. Hicks, who knew everything about the village—perhaps April could bring up the subject while they continued the inventory after breakfast.

Petteril breezed in, still in his riding clothes. "Good morning, my lady."

"Good morning, my lord." She eyed him as he sat down, sensing the thrum of excitement radiating from his person. "You are big with news," she guessed.

"Indubitably. I'll tell you after breakfast. If Mr. Pepper has not yet arrived."

"Mr. Pepper will wait," she said firmly. "He can be plied with tea and breakfast. In fact, I suspect he should be if he has travelled on the night mail coach. When will we be able to go to the inn again?"

"This afternoon, perhaps."

April finished her food in record time and gazed at him expectantly.

"Have another cup of coffee," he invited, reaching for the pot. "I shan't be long."

She eyed him threateningly. "I will get my own back, you know?"

He laughed and gave in, swallowing the last of his coffee. "Come then. We'll go to your sitting room."

She didn't ask why not his. Stewart was likely to be there.

Unfortunately, Mrs. Hicks, in the absence of a lady's maid, was tidying up in April's apartments.

"Thank you, Mrs. Hicks," Petteril said. "Her ladyship will join you presently."

Mrs. Hicks, surprisingly, obeyed with alacrity. She even blushed, much to April's amazement—and amusement, until she realized what the housekeeper imagined.

How sad that it was not true.

Shame burned April's face. "Well?" she said aggressively, to cover her feelings.

Petteril went to the low table. He put his hand in his pocket and drew out a small, fat leather purse. Loosening the strings, he emptied a pile of coins and rolled up bank notes.

April's jaw dropped. "Cor! Is that…? Where was it?"

"Yes, I think it is." He raked through the pile. "Ten or so guineas in coins and, yes, fifty pounds in bank notes." He scooped them all back into the purse and pocketed it. "I found it buried at the folly. Almost directly behind where Stewart was sitting last night."

"Oh, no." She raised both hands to her face in distress. "He buried it there?"

"It does seem likeliest," Petteril said. "Though in theory, anyone else could have brought it from the inn and buried it, including whoever was with Stewart last night."

April sat down on the sofa. "What are you going to do?"

"I'm not sure yet. I need to speak to Pepper, and I most definitely need to speak to Stewart himself."

"Don't you have to give the purse to the magistrate?"

"Probably. For now, I had better change for our reading class. Could you look after Mr. Pepper, if he arrives?"

"Yes, of course," she said without thought. Her mind was all on Stewart. No one was as they seemed. *It still might not be him…* And if Stewart truly was a thief, could he really have tried to shoot his lordship just to prevent him finding out?

Chapter Nine

When Captain Vincent Lyall had wakened that morning, he could not at first work out why he felt so cheerful. His arm was still missing, irritating him with an impossible itch that could not be scratched. His leg still ached abominably. And he still had to go home and face the pity of his family, and a lifetime of relying on their resources rather than his own.

And yet something very like hope had driven him out of bed to begin the ridiculously long rigmarole of washing and dressing himself. He could not prevent the sense of sweet anticipation because he would most probably see *her* again.

And because she made him realize he did not have to give in to his misfortune. His life was not over because he had been wounded in war. So had thousands of other poor sods, left considerably less able, or lost their lives altogether. Including friends. They had all accepted the dangers of war, and Lyall was one of the lucky ones.

He had learned a great deal in his years in the army. He just had to find another way to put his knowledge to use. Much more productive than self-pity and envy of the able-bodied. Plus, he had a start, he remembered. A little money he did not *have* to fritter away on wine and wagers. He was not so ill a specimen.

He fastened the last of his uniform buttons, gave his hair a cursory brush, and left his bedchamber. There she was.

"Good morning, sir," Verity greeted him with a shy smile, as she carried a plateful of bacon and eggs and sausages from the kitchen.

He smiled back. "Good morning." Despite her bright greeting, she looked tired, as though she had slept poorly and had too much on her mind. He wondered if he could help.

In the meantime, he limped after her across the room, his heart thudding as if he were going into battle.

He bowed. "Miss Camden. Good morning."

She smiled and a pleasant fizz of awareness coursed through his veins. "Good morning, Captain. Will you join me? I'm sure Verity counts as a chaperone."

Verity smiled in a rather perfunctory way as she placed the breakfast plate before the lady. "Coffee and breakfast, sir?"

"Thank you." He eased himself into the chair opposite Miss Camden. "Is Sir Darius well enough to come down today?"

"I believe he means to come down, just to test the waters, you understand. He is feeling much more the thing."

"I'm glad to hear it. Please, eat your breakfast before it gets cold."

She began to eat, and Verity poured him a cup of coffee. He picked it up and regarded Miss Camden over the rim.

"I was thinking of riding over to Haybury Court this afternoon, perhaps call on the Petterils. Would you and Sir Darius care to accompany me?"

"I would," she replied. "Though I cannot speak for Darius. It is a pleasant ride to the Court, which looks to be a very fine house from the outside."

"You have been there already?" he asked, surprised.

"Oh, just hacking, you know."

"It does look very grand," Lyall admitted. "Complete with a ruined chapel."

"Ah, you noticed that, too! Very Gothic. Although I believe it's a folly built a mere half-century ago to add character. Still, I would like to look at it more closely."

"So would I," Lyall said. And only then noticed that Sir Darius was striding toward him, scowling furiously.

PIERS WALKED INTO HIS office to discover Mr. Pepper already ensconced in a comfortable chair by the desk with a cup of tea and a plate of fresh scones at his elbow. He was sorting through documents spread out on Piers's desk, though he rose at once and bowed, beaming with apparent pleasure.

"Welcome, Mr. Pepper," Piers said, holding out his hand. "I hope your journey wasn't too awful."

"Surprisingly comfortable." Pepper shook hands enthusiastically. "Or at least quick. May I offer you my felicitations, my lord? My compliments to the new viscountess."

"Thank you. You shall meet her later, no doubt. May I not order you something more substantial than scones?"

"No, no, I breakfasted in Blanchester. This is perfect. So, to business. This is the marriage settlement I have drawn up, and your will. I believe I have included everything you mentioned in your letter but let us go over them."

Piers settled into the opposite chair and prepared for an hour or so of boredom. He had to remind himself that April's future security could depend on his paying attention, otherwise his mind would have drifted off. Legal language usually sent him straight to sleep.

An hour later, satisfied, he was happy to sign both documents. Barlow and Patrick, the first footman, were summoned to witness his signature, and then sent back to their duties.

"There is another matter I wish to discuss with you," Piers said, helping the solicitor to gather his documents together. "Though you may not carry the answers in your head. The servants you found for me in London—I am assuming they all came with good characters?"

"Indeed. Though to be fair, I don't believe I found more than Mr. and Mrs. Park for you. They engaged most of the other servants. I did, however, write to the previous employers of everyone, just to be sure."

"That's what I thought," said Piers, who actually had paid very little attention to the whole process. He had not wanted a personal servant and it had irked him that a valet was considered necessary to his new status. Stewart, however, never got in his way and somehow had become invaluable very quickly. "Do you remember who Stewart, my valet, worked for previously?"

"Actually, yes, for he was young for the position, and I made a point of writing. A young Scottish gentleman called Ross who employed him for about two years. He spoke very highly of Stewart, and only let him go because he was about to travel to Canada and didn't know when he would return."

Piers nodded. "I don't suppose you know what he did before serving this Mr. Ross?"

"I don't believe he was in service. Why do you ask? Is the man not giving satisfaction?"

"There was an incident," Piers said reluctantly. "He was accused of theft, and I wish to clear his name, only once one starts looking, there is always more to people than one assumes."

Pepper was outraged. "You think he did it? Have your own things gone missing?"

"No, never. And I don't believe he stole Sir Darius's purse either. Apart from anything else, I can't imagine he would be so stupid." Frowning, Piers drummed his fingers on the documents beneath them. "Would you do me a favour, Mr. Pepper? Could you stay here tonight and advise me of the law, if necessary?"

"I shall certainly do my best."

"Thank you." He reached out and pulled the bell behind him. "Treat the house as your own. There is a very decent library and some pleasant walks if you feel like stretching your legs after being cramped in a coach all night. Or rest if you would rather... Ah, Patrick, show Mr. Pepper to a guest bedchamber and have his bags taken up, would you?"

"Certainly, my lord. This way, sir."

Piers placed his will and one copy of the marriage settlement in the safe cupboard, which he locked. Then he picked the remaining copy off his desk and went in search of April.

He eventually found her in the dining room with Mrs. Hicks, gazing with awe at a collection of seventeenth century silver cutlery, which had been stashed out of the way in the bottom drawer of a sideboard.

"Have you seen this?" she asked, raising a tarnished spoon in wonder.

"Actually, I'm not sure I have. I don't recall it ever being used."

"Can we use it?"

"We can use anything you like."

"I like these."

"Then use them for your first dinner party if you like. May I drag you away for a little?"

"Of course," she said at once, dropping the spoon back in the drawer.

"I'll have the set polished," Mrs. Hicks said comfortably.

In the library, April sat stony-faced through his explanation of the settlement. "You mean I get Sillitrees once you're dead?"

"Yes. For your lifetime."

"What would I want with Sillitrees?"

"I thought you liked it there."

"I do."

"Well, you'll need somewhere to live, because Haybury is entailed and will be the home of whoever succeeds me as viscount. There will also be funds enough for you to live comfortably."

"I won't live comfortably if you're dead," she said flatly.

"I'm not planning on it just yet," he said, aiming for humour. "There is also an allowance, payable now and for the rest of your life."

She stared at him, two angry spots forming on her cheeks. "I don't want your money."

"I never supposed you did. It's a perk. For being the viscountess. It means you can buy what you would like without consulting me, whether clothes or books, jewels or horses. And there is a separate budget for household expenses."

"I thought you were hard-up," she muttered.

"The estate is not yet what it once was, but all things are relative. We are not poor."

She opened her mouth and closed it again. She was still angry, but he guessed she didn't know why. He did. She didn't want to think of his death. And beyond a safe place and the bizarre friendship they had formed from the first, she had never wanted anything of him.

"I've got nothing to give you," she said.

He frowned and she met his gaze.

"When I die," she explained. "I'll have nothing to give you. Nothing that you haven't given me first."

"Yes, you will. You give to me every day." Half-embarrassed by his own words, he swung away to the door, adding hastily. "That is your copy. I have another and so does Pepper. And now, I think, I should go and find Stewart."

In fact, he almost cannoned into Stewart, who was emerging in a huge rush from the viscount's apartments.

The valet fell back immediately, holding the door. "My lord."

"Ah, Stewart. Did you see my riding coat?"

"I have just brushed off the mud and put it away."

"Did you see the tear in the right seam?"

Stewart's lips tightened. It was a rare mistake. "I'm afraid I didn't." He followed Piers back into the room. "I'll give it to Mrs. Hicks to have it sewn."

They went together to the wardrobe, and Stewart took down the riding coat. From its lopsided hang, the purse remained in its pocket.

Stewart's brow twitched into a frown. His mind was clearly not on his work today. He delved into the pocket and brought out the purse.

He was about to lay it on the chest of drawers when he froze, staring at the purse in clear shock.

Piers's heart sank.

"It isn't mine," he said. "But I see you recognize it."

Stewart swallowed. "I think it's Sir Darius's missing purse."

And how would you know that if you had never seen it? "I could make you guess where I found it, but it's not a game I want to play. Did you bury it?"

Stewart nodded once. The silence stretched intolerably, but Piers refused to break it.

"I don't expect you to believe me," Stewart said at last, "but I didn't steal it."

"Then how did it fall into your hands?"

"Someone gave it to me."

"Who?"

"I'm afraid I can't tell you that."

"But you hid it anyway, knowing it was stolen?"

Stewart nodded again. "Stupid, really. I should have known you would find it. It just seemed safer than bringing it into the house."

"When did you bury it? Last night?"

Stewart glanced at him, hesitating. Then: "No. Tuesday night."

"The night it was stolen. Obstructing justice is a crime."

"I know."

"But right now, on the evidence, they would be justified in trying you for theft."

"I know that, too. I'm sorry."

"I believe you," Piers said, eying him through his quizzing glass. "Though exactly what you are sorry for eludes me. Who are you protecting?"

"I can't tell you that, my lord."

"You want me to guess?"

"No, sir."

"Bad luck. I'm going to. It must be either a woman or an old friend."

Stewart's gaze flickered again, but it told Petteril nothing.

"Which means Miss Camden, the maidservant Verity Small, Neil Murray, or whatever stranger blew my hat off with a pistol ball."

Stewart looked him in the eye. An odd little smile twitched across his lips and vanished. "You won't give up either, will you? That was always one of the things I admired in you. I don't suppose you would give me a few hours start before you inform the magistrate?"

"You suppose correctly. You had much better tell me the truth."

"I can't."

"Then let me guess again. Neil Murray is no friend of yours, though perhaps he once was, and so you feel compelled to keep quiet over his misdeeds."

"Oh, no, I'll tell you about those. He's a nasty little shite. If you'll forgive my language. In fact, I'm on my way to the inn now to teach him a lesson."

"No you aren't. Sit."

Reluctantly, Stewart sat on the couch along the wall, the riding coat clutched across his lap. Petteril settled in the armchair.

"Did Murray steal the purse from Sir Darius's room?"

Stewart hesitated, then shook his head. "No," he said regretfully. "But he *is* a thief, and I would be happy enough to see him imprisoned for it. Or hanged, preferably."

"How do you know he's a thief?" Piers asked.

Stewart met his gaze steadily. "Because I am one, too."

VERITY COULD NOT AVOID cleaning Murray's room. It was part of her duties. And there was always a small chance she would be able to retrieve her letter while she was there. Not that she truly thought Murray would be so careless as to leave it lying around, but he would not be the first man to underestimate her.

Choosing her moment when she was sure he had gone out, she unlocked his door and went inside with her duster and brush. She smoothed the sheets and spread up the bed quickly, feeling under the pillows and inside their cases for anything that should not be there. She even swept a hand under the mattress but found nothing. Then she emptied the chamber pot into her covered pail, and swept the floor, allowing herself a further peek under the furniture as she did so.

Finally, she flicked a duster around the chest of drawers and was just wondering if she dared look inside when she heard footsteps on the stairs. *Murray.*

She hurried to the door, grabbing her broom, bucket, and dustpan as she went.

It was almost inevitable that they should meet in the doorway.

"Ah, Verity. Spick and span as ever," he said, beaming. His smile never touched his eyes. It was as if someone had taught him the movement but not the reason. "Do you have something for me? Or is it something you must deliver later?"

"I haven't decided," she said desperately. "Give me until the end of the day."

Something touched his eyes, then—not a smile but it looked like pleasurable lust. She felt sick.

"Funnily enough," Murray said, "that suits me perfectly."

"TELL ME," PIERS SAID.

Stewart sighed. "It's not an edifying story, and it's not unique. I had a wild youth, from the age of about fifteen—reaction, perhaps to my strict upbringing. My father was a minister with a small congregation and a large family. I stopped going to school without his knowledge, to roam the streets in town looking for amusement. I found it with other lads who seemed to have no boundaries, no lines of right and wrong, but they did have fun."

He shifted on the couch, his fist clenching around the riding coat. "I won't bore you with the details. Suffice it to say, I was in bad company and I liked it. I graduated quickly from drinking what I couldn't afford to helping myself. I moved on to a larger town, and then Edinburgh, where I lived with a crowd of equally wild boys and girls by means of petty theft."

"This was when you learned to fight in tavern brawls," Piers guessed.

"Yes."

"Came in very handy at the Queen's Head. Was this when you met Murray too?"

Stewart curled his lip. "He fancied himself as a master criminal, but frankly, he never had the brains. But he thought big, and I, pretty much drunk all the time, went along with it. Three of us stole a cart from outside a warehouse in Leith. It was loaded with—" He broke off, shrugging impatiently. "It doesn't matter now. For me, the important thing was that we attacked a man to get it—the driver or guard or whatever he was. I told myself we fought him for it, but it wasn't much of a fight. There were three of us and he wasn't expecting it right outside the door."

Stewart's face was a grim line. "I still see him in my nightmares. Bloody. Unconscious."

"Was he dead?" Piers asked steadily.

"No, but he wasn't going to be working for a good few weeks, which was pretty much a death sentence for him and his family. And for me, it was like that blinding light on the road to Damascus, only there was no joy in it. I saw what I had become, what I *would* become, and I was terrified."

"What became of the goods you stole?"

"They were sold, of course. I got my share. I nearly threw it back in Murray's face."

"What *did* you do with it?" Piers asked.

Stewart waved one derisive hand. "Too little and too late. But I found out where that man lived—the one we hurt—and dropped the money into his wife's apron when I passed her in the street."

Dropped the money into his wife's apron. Piers's mind grasped those words, an elusive idea forming for later.

"I never went back to my den of thieves," Stewart said.

"Did you go home?"

"I was too ashamed. I found bits and pieces of work in Edinburgh, eventually with a tailor who let me sleep in the back of the shop. He was a good tailor, got a lot of wealthy custom, which is how I met Mr. Ross, a gentleman not much older than me. I amused him, I think, because I was educated; something from school or my father's teachings must have stuck in my brain after all. He took me on as his valet and we went to London together."

Stewart's eyes refocused on Piers. "I never saw Murray again until the Red Lion on Tuesday."

"What did he want?"

"Blackmail. He knew I worked for you and couldn't afford my past to come out."

"Why did you go up to his room? Was he really that bosky?"

"No. I wanted to be private with him."

"To pay him off?"

"And to scare the wits out of him. I told him if he ever asked for more money, if he ever came near me again, I'd kill him."

"Did he believe you?" Piers asked.

"Oh yes," Stewart said with satisfaction.

And there again was the brawler from the Queen's Head. Stewart must have been quite a scary youth.

"Then why," Piers asked, "did you tell me you were going to the inn to teach him a lesson? Another lesson, one presumes."

Stewart hesitated.

"You're not the only one he's blackmailing, are you?" Piers said.

Stewart shook his head. "It's like breathing to him. Everyone he encounters is a potential source of gain."

"Do you think he set you up to take the blame for Sir Darius's theft? Since you'd no doubt convinced him he'd get no more blunt out of you."

"No, though he wasn't above pointing the magistrate in my direction, insisting I'd only been in his room a minute when I disappeared from the taproom for ten."

"To sit on the stairs and think," Piers said without emphasis.

"I'm surprised *you* find that odd."

"Oh, it isn't odd for me," Piers said vaguely. He stood, pacing across to the door and back. "Is someone in danger at the Red Lion?"

"Possibly."

"Then don't you think you should let Lady Petteril and me sort it out?"

Stewart stared at him. "Am I not dismissed?"

"No, damn it. I told you, I'm used to you, and you've been a good friend to us both. But this theft accusation won't go away if you rush about beating people up. Why is Murray going to London?"

"Probably to get away from the law in Scotland."

"That's what I—"

A knock at the outer door interrupted him. Without a word, Stewart rose and walked through to the sitting room to answer. Piers followed more slowly, emerging in time to see Stewart closing the sitting room door once more.

The valet looked worried. "Mr. Lindon is here."

Chapter Ten

April had the dizzying feeling that her life was swirling out of control.

Living in a big house, despite the shock and the novelty, had never frightened her or overwhelmed her, because her main focus had never been the house or the wealth or the titled, pampered people who drifted in and out. It had always been *him*, Lord Petteril.

The realization that she was mistress of Haybury Court, and Sillitrees, and a smart London town house—and no doubt lesser properties too—was slow to sink in. It had taken the document in her hand to ram it home. She was a wealthy woman for the rest of her life. She, the thief from the gutters of St. Giles.

Even without Lord Petteril, if he died, she would be rich. She would always have a home, something she had dreamed of on her sawdust bed in the corner of the Silver Jug taproom, with only a mangy dog for company. She hoped Tatty remembered to feed that dog...

The change in her circumstances was suddenly overwhelming, no less so because it would mean nothing without *him*.

She had not achieved this wealth. She did not deserve it. This was no success. The only success she cared about was making him happy and yet he was still elusive, still stressed enough to sleep badly and go out at dawn to fight his devils. If anything, that had grown worse since coming home.

That would be a success, a victory, she thought. *If only I could make him happy enough to rest, to sleep into the morning...*

"My lady," Patrick the footman said from the library door, and she almost laughed to realize he was talking to her.

Madness, utter madness. She should be used to it by now. "Yes?"

"Mr. and Mrs. Lindon have called, wondering if you are receiving yet."

"Oh. Of course," she said. "Show them to the drawing room, Patrick, and bring tea, will you?"

Only when Patrick had gone did she panic.

The last time she had seen the Lindons, some five months ago, their lives were in tatters, and she had been Lord Petteril's assistant, doubling as a maid. That Mrs. Lindon called on her at all meant she had no idea that the assistant was now the viscountess. April could almost see the woman's nostrils flaring with contempt and disgust at first sight of her.

But perhaps the visit was nothing to do with her. Lindon could be here as magistrate. He could have come for Stewart. The stolen purse swam past through her mind.

But that was silly. He would hardly have brought his wife with him to arrest Lord Petteril's manservant!

Nervously, she patted her hair and straightened her gown, and wished cravenly that his lordship was with her.

Well, she'd been alone before and in a lot worse situations than this. When she had first agreed to marry him, she had told him that she could take the contempt from his world if Petteril himself could face the ridicule. It was true. Only somehow, now it was upon her, it didn't seem quite so easy.

But, for him, she could be the viscountess.

Lifting her head, she sailed out of the library and along the gracious gallery to the drawing room.

Mr. Lindon leapt to his feet at once. Mrs. Lindon, who hadn't been sitting, curtseyed.

"Mrs. Lindon," April said, walking toward her, waiting resignedly for the lady's avid, smiling expression to change to appalled recognition.

"Lady Petteril? How charming of you to receive us! I know it is a little soon for a bride visit, but his lordship is such an old friend, we hoped you wouldn't mind."

"I am very glad to see you," April said, looking her in the eye.

April offered her hand, still smiling, and Mrs. Lindon pressed it between both of hers.

"Why, how lovely you are! Isn't she, Robert? Oh, allow me to present my husband, Mr. Lindon. He is the squire, you know, and also the magistrate in these parts."

April gave Mr. Lindon her hand, too, but though his eyes gleamed in appreciation, he did not appear to recognize her either.

What did she do now? Simply announce, *I used to be April, Lord Petteril's assistant. You know, the maid who helped at your ball in the spring?*

"We've been looking forward very much to meeting you," Mr. Lindon said, smiling. "And I have to say Petteril is a dashed lucky fellow. How do you do, my lady? So delightful to have a bright young lady in the neighbourhood. We have been missing our daughter, who is recently married and so moved south with her husband."

"You're very kind," April said, indicating they should sit. "How is Lady Maxwell?"

Even this large hint that she knew their family seemed to miss its mark.

"Ah, his lordship has told you all about us!" Mrs. Lindon said, clearly gratified, and yet with a hint of fear behind her eyes.

She didn't want her family to be known to the new viscountess merely for the tragedies and scandals of the spring. Which made April pause and consider.

"I'm afraid your peace and quiet is probably over," Mrs. Lindon continued brightly, perhaps to distract her. "Now that we have called, you will have all your neighbours begging to greet the bride!"

"Naturally, they will be welcome," April said, trying not to sound nervous.

"How are you settling in at Haybury Court?" Lindon asked kindly.

"Oh, finding my feet," April said. "It is a large responsibility."

"We hope you'll be very happy here," said Mrs. Lindon with a sincerity that took April rather by surprise. She had not really cared for Mrs. Lindon before, finding her shallow and socially too ambitious for comfort. To say nothing of the flirting.

"Thank you, I know I will be," April said, though she knew no such thing. For a moment, in her mind, Petteril was already dead, and she was being packed off to Sillitrees. She blinked the vision away, just as Lord Petteril strolled into the room.

April breathed again as he and the Lindons greeted each other cordially. The tea things were brought in right behind him, so April could busy herself with pouring tea. Petteril, being the amiable host, carried a cup to Mrs. Lindon, and Mavis offered plates of scones and honey cakes.

It was clearly a social call, for no one mentioned the theft at the Red Lion or Stewart, and when Miss Camden and Captain Lyall were announced, April had grown relaxed enough to take it in her stride. She found a novel pleasure in playing hostess, keeping her guests supplied with tea and biscuits.

No doubt inspired by the captain's presence, the conversation turned to military events on the peninsula.

Captain Lyall grew tight-lipped at Mr. Lindon's criticism. "Wellington will do what is necessary."

"I find the news from Russia more worrying," Lord Petteril said, deflecting argument. "Despite a major battle with great losses, I believe the French still advance upon Moscow."

Mrs. Lindon shuddered. "Bonaparte is a monster."

"He is an ingenious monster," Lyall said. "I would like to see him come up against Wellington in person."

Mr. Lindon looked disparaging.

"More tea, Miss Camden?" April said brightly. A good hostess avoided disagreements among her guests, which was a pity for she found this subject much more interesting than the weather. She suspected from her wry smile that Miss Camden did too.

April knew from Petteril that even in the country, which was less exacting than town, a polite caller did not overstay their welcome. So she was not surprised when Mrs. Lindon stood to take her leave.

Since the visit had passed off extraordinarily well, considering, April chose to push the matter by accompanying the Lindons downstairs to their waiting carriage. She more than half-expected one or both of them to turn on her, accusing her of low-birth and inveigling a good man into a disastrous marriage.

Instead, as she pulled on her gloves in the entrance hall, Mrs. Lindon lowered her voice confidingly. "I know you have lived abroad, so I hope you don't mind my warning you against Miss Camden."

April blinked. "Really? I didn't know you knew her."

"Oh, I don't personally, but she is clearly Sir Darius Camden's sister, so she is the one."

"What one?" April asked mystified.

Mrs. Lindon touched her lips. "Scandal. She ran away with some unsuitable man who abandoned her. She was quite ruined, and yet there she sits in your drawing room, daring to call on you, escorted by yet another man she is not married to nor related to. I know you won't want to make a friend of such a creature. I would cut her, if I were you. Goodbye, Lady Petteril, so wonderful to have met you."

Mr. Lindon was herding her out of the door, though he paused to bow once more over April's hand, before hurrying after his wife.

Thoughtfully, April waved from the front step before returning to her apparently scandalous guests. She rather liked Miss Camden. More, she sympathized with anyone who was a victim of scandal in this strange world of Petteril's, so full of rigid rules and expectations. Though if Captain Lyall was her lover—would-be lover might be more exact—April couldn't help wondering why she would have come to the folly last night to meet Stewart.

"How progresses your investigation, my lord?" Miss Camden was asking as April returned to the drawing room. "Have you managed to clear your manservant in the eyes of the law?"

"I have a few ideas," Petteril said vaguely, rising as April entered.

She still valued the courtesy, although she signalled to both him and Captain Lyall to be seated.

"And what is this business about someone shooting your hat?" Miss Camden demanded.

"Another good question," Lord Petteril said, "to which I do not yet have the answer. Will you allow me to ask *you* something? Both of you?"

Captain Lyall nodded. April picked up the teapot and refilled his cup. Miss Camden shook her head with a quick smile. She looked suddenly, uncharacteristically nervous.

"It comes down to opportunity," Petteril said. "Which is made all the more difficult by the fact that Sir Darius is a somewhat disorganized and forgetful gentleman. Or perhaps you disagree, Miss Camden? You know him best."

"No, I could not disagree. Your description is accurate, if only a part of who he is."

"While he was in the taproom on Tuesday night," Petteril said, "I don't suppose you went into his chamber?"

"He locked it," Miss Camden said at once. Then, with a quick smile. "Or so he thinks. I did not try. And I did not steal my brother's money."

"Of course not!" Petteril sounded shocked. April knew him well enough to know that he was not. "My query was really to establish the whereabouts of the purse. Is it possible Sir Darius had it with him at the taproom and forgot about it?"

"Quite possible," Miss Camden said ruefully.

Petteril turned to Captain Lyall. "If you think back to that night, did you see Sir Darius take out the purse? Did he pay for his drink with coin?"

Lyall blinked. "I really wasn't paying attention. I have no idea."

"His normal habit at inns and hostelries," Miss Camden put in, "is to pay the whole shot when he departs."

"Hmm," Petteril acknowledged, turning back to Lyall. "Was anyone drinking with him? At his table?"

Lyall frowned, thinking about it. "No, the locals kept to themselves pretty much. I'm too grumpy to drink with anyone else and Murray was on his own too."

"Then did anyone go near him at any point?" Petteril asked.

"Tucker, I suppose, to bring him another drink."

But Tucker never left the taproom, April thought. "Did he have supper there?" she asked.

"He likes to eat," Miss Camden acknowledged.

Lyall scowled. "I really have no... Actually, yes, he did. The maidservant, Verity, brought him a bowl of stew."

"You didn't see him pay for it?" Petteril said without much hope.

"No, but I wasn't observing him. I imagine it went on his shot with the drinks. Barnes would no doubt be able to tell you."

Petteril sighed. "Yes, I really need to speak to Barnes. Perhaps I'll drop in to the inn later. Tell me, what's your opinion of Mr. Murray?"

Miss Camden's expression never changed, but her fingers in her lap tightened, whitening her knuckles.

Interesting...

"Don't know him," Lyall said flatly.

"But you are used to judging men, Captain," April said, switching her attention. "Would he make a good soldier?"

"I don't know him," Lyall repeated. "He's fit enough, intelligent enough. But I doubt he follows orders well. He seems the type to have the men at each other's throats just by the odd word flung into the wrong place. But I have no proof of that. He just reminds me of..." He shrugged impatiently, as though shaking off memories of the life he had left behind.

"Do you share that impression, Miss Camden?" April asked.

"I do. These scones are delicious, Lady Petteril. My compliments to your cook."

"WHAT DO YOU MAKE OF them?" April murmured as they waved off Miss Camden and Captain Lyall, mounted and trotting off down the drive together. They made a handsome couple. From his straight back, one wouldn't have guessed the captain's injury.

"I'd say they are both discontented."

"But not with each other," April said. "I'd say she is good for him. On the other hand..." She lowered her voice. "Mrs. Lindon has just told me there is some scandal in Miss Camden's past. She is apparently ruined in society. She—Mrs. Lindon—even advised me to cut her. She seems to have forgotten her own scandal."

"Well, we covered it up," Petteril murmured. "What did Miss Camden do?"

"Eloped, apparently, and was abandoned."

"Interesting."

"Why?"

"Blackmail," Petteril said, turning and going back into the house.

Aware of the servants, April managed to bite her lip only until they were inside the library.

"It's all about blackmail?" she demanded, as soon as he had shut the door.

"I think so. I spoke to Stewart, who finally admitted that Murray was blackmailing him—Stewart's past being somewhat unsavoury and his present dependent on respectability."

"Tell me," April said, intrigued in spite of herself. She listened carefully while Petteril told her about his conversation with his valet, both what he confessed and what he refused to say. Her fingers itched for the notebook shut up in her sitting room drawer. "Doesn't seem so very bad to me," she said hopefully. "No worse than me, at any rate, just on a slightly bigger scale and he's clearly reformed."

"I wasn't about to dismiss him," Petteril said mildly.

April smiled with a hint of relief. "Didn't think you were. So Murray's the villain. Yet according to Stewart, he didn't take Sir Darius's purse. How does he know that?"

"Because he knows who did take it."

"Who?"

"One of the other blackmail victims, I imagine. To pay Murray off."

Petteril sat in his favourite chair, and without thinking, April knelt at his feet. Her breath caught, but either he didn't notice or he didn't mind, for he didn't send her to the chair opposite, a much more decorous position.

"Who?" April wondered. "How many victims does he have?"

"At least two. Stewart and whoever he is so furious to protect. Which *might* be Miss Camden."

"Then he didn't tell you who was with him at the folly last night?"

"He did not. But whatever the mistakes of his youth, he has a strong sense of honour and a code he won't break."

April nodded. "He gave his share of the robbery to the man they injured."

"Dropped it into her apron pocket," Petteril said. "Aprons can be very useful."

"So she'd never know." April threw back her head in frustration. "Trouble is, everyone has secrets. Might not be horrible ones like mine and Stewart's and poor Miss Camden's, but most people surely have something they don't want to be public knowledge, even for the sake of embarrassment. Just wait until he gets a whiff of *my* past."

"Well, he would have no joy there, since I already know and those of the neighbourhood who haven't worked it out already soon will—at least as far as April the assistant."

They lapsed into silence, each thinking in silence, until April became aware of his knee so close to her. Greatly daring, she laid her head against it. Her heart skittered with fear and the intimacy made her close her eyes. How long would he give her? Two seconds? Three?

Absently, his hand stroked her hair and fear dissolved into wonder.

"There is also the question of the shot," he said. "Which could have been Lyall. For all we know, he has deserted or been cashiered for some crime. If Murray discovered that, it would be a gift."

"And the captain does not appear to be a rich man," April agreed. Beneath her cheek, his knee was warm and hard and very still. "Could he have taken the purse to pay Murray off?"

"And then tried to kill Murray? Makes no sense. But he could have tried to kill him *instead* of paying him."

"He was taking a risk with so many other people close by—especially you."

"And frankly, he seems ill and injured enough to account for his return to England," Petteril said. "I doubt he is the dishonourable kind." His hand stilled but did not leave her. It lay light and sweet against the back of her head. "Nor is Miss Camden, and though they began walking separately that morning, they said they returned to the inn together to find everyone debating the shooting."

"Then you still think it was a stranger?"

"A stranger to us, but not necessarily to Murray. We need to find out the truth about him as well as the theft." His hand shifted absently to the sensitive skin of her nape and she forgot to breathe. "And," he added thoughtfully, "we might need a way to get rid of Murray without revealing the secrets of his victims."

His fingers, sending delicious little thrills through her veins, paused, then slid away. "I think I need to speak to Brandy Bill."

She lifted her head, blinking at him. Brandy Bill was a highwayman—retired—who had married the nurse of Lord Petteril's late cousins and lived in a village between here and Blanchester.

"You can't think Bill would have anything to do with this? His wife would cut off—"

"Quite," Petteril agreed, springing to his feet. "But I'll lay you any money you like that Bill keeps a close eye on who enters the area, if only to know who to avoid. Our man has to be somewhere. And he's likely to try again."

"That's what I thought. I'll come with you."

"Very..." He broke off, and turned back, frowning. "Actually... I think one of us needs to stay here to stop Stewart haring off to the inn for vengeance against Murray. If that happens, neither of us could save him from the noose."

She could see the sense in it. Still... "Why don't I go and talk to Brandy Bill, then? You've got more chance of keeping Stewart in line. And besides, if you went to the inn with him, you might be able to find out who took the purse."

"I'm pretty sure I know that already," he said and closed the door behind him.

Outrage kept her still for several long, fuming moments. By the time she'd bolted to the top of the stairs, he had already gone. She almost swore after him, but a footman was crossing the hall.

Chapter Eleven

Brandy Bill, now the respectable Mr. William Brandon, husband of the Withan family's old retainer Mrs. Gardener, greeted Piers like a long lost friend.

He was, Piers reflected, making quite a collection of reformed criminals among his intimates. Bill now looked after the small holding his wife had inherited from her late husband, and had a sideline in healing sick animals, with the help of Mrs. Brandon's herbal potions. She was delighted to see Piers, her old favourite of the family, and happily fed him tea and sandwiches and cake while she demanded to know all about his new wife.

"You know her," Piers said. "My assistant, April."

Mrs. Brandon's mouth fell open. She swallowed. "Was that wise?" she managed.

"Wisest thing I ever did," Piers assured her.

"Doesn't she find it...difficult?"

"Yes. But I've never come across anyone so adaptable."

"But is she..." Mrs. Brandon struggled. "Accepted?"

"By the servants? So far, though admittedly they may just be flabbergasted. By society—who knows? Mrs. Lindon invited her to tea. I don't propose to inflict the ton upon her."

"Well!" Mrs. Brandon exhaled noisily, then, rather to his surprise, glared at him. "You look after that girl. She's devoted to you."

Heat seeped into his cheeks. *Is she?* At least he didn't speak the wistful thought aloud. There was a difference between her odd friendship mingled with gratitude and the kind of devotion he wanted so badly—and had promised to eschew.

Was it pathetic to hope just because she did not flinch when he touched her? It was still miles short of...

He dragged his mind back to the reason he was here. "I'll bring her to visit you," he promised. "Today, I really came to pick Bill's brain."

Mrs. Brandon opened her mouth, then closed it again. "Got a few things to do," she announced and departed.

Bill watched her fondly. "She's a fine woman."

"She is indeed. I'm glad to see things going so well for you both."

Bill beamed. "What can I do for your lordship?"

"I don't suppose you know anything about villains in Scotland? Edinburgh and Leith in particular."

"Can't say I do." Bill scratched his chin. "Didn't really mix much with the fraternity, to be honest. Kept myself to myself. And Scotland's a long way off."

"True. Then, tell me, have you noticed any strangers in the area recently, perhaps Scottish strangers, asking questions about another Scot?"

Bill cocked an intelligent eyebrow. "You think they're the law?"

"I'm wondering if they're thieves diddled by a Scotsman called Murray. Or even decent but desperate men sick of his blackmail."

Bill hesitated. He had always been too open to be a successful highwayman. "Some men you just shouldn't get on the wrong side of."

"Peer of the realm," Piers said, flicking imaginary dust from his sleeve. "Some men would worry more about that. Besides, can't go on having my hat shot off in my own village."

Bill looked startled, then stood up. "Better get my pistol then," he said resignedly. "And we'll go for a pint at the local."

"Um...best leave the pistol," Piers suggested. "It doesn't make a good drinking companion."

The local inn was only a few steps away. Piers used the time to discover how long the stranger concerned had been staying there.

"Saw him arrive on Wednesday evening," Bill said. "Didn't give a reason, just paid up in advance. Lying low, I thought at the time. And he sounds Scottish. Looks like the kind of cove used to put the fear of God into other coves."

"Like a debt collector?"

"Probably. But what kind of debts?"

Piers took the point.

In his riding clothes, he stood out among the local farmers and labourers. He found himself drawing on another persona, an icily ruthless gentleman who was no gentleman, and who retained some of the qualities of his old St. Giles role of dangerous clerk and forger.

"Corner," Bill murmured. "Alone, finishing his pint. Looks about to leave. Ale?" Bill nodded toward a free table near the door.

"Brandy," Piers said and, ignoring Bill's direction, went and sat at his quarry's table.

He kept his expression cold and distant when the Scotsman glared at him for daring to sit so close. He even met the man's gaze. It was not a comforting experience. The man's eyes were vaguely inhuman, as if no one lived behind them. No empathy, no compassion. And yet it was the Scot who looked away first, even if his lip curled into a sneer.

"There you go, sir," Bill said, setting down the brandy and his own ale. He nodded to the Scot in civil recognition. "Evening."

The stranger did not reply.

Piers sipped his brandy.

The Scotsman began to rise.

"I believe you're looking for an acquaintance of mine," Piers said.

The man stared at him. "Shouldn't think so."

It was a risk, but Piers put his cards on the table. "Name of Neil Murray."

The Scotsman sat back down.

SINCE LORD PETTERIL was riding all the way to the Brandons' cottage, April didn't really expect him back for dinner. On the other hand, she doubted Stewart would risk his employment further by being absent when his lordship came home to change.

From the time she had first worked for Lord Petteril, Stewart had been a solid if generally silent ally in the servants' halls of the viscount's homes. When she had been promoted to "assistant", it was Stewart who, almost single-handedly, had nipped any salacious gossip in the bud and ensured she was given at least outward respect until she could prove herself. She rather missed their occasional exchanges. It was all different now. She had sacrificed her few friends to be Lady Petteril.

Impulsively, once changed for dinner as was expected of her, she changed direction, and instead of going straight downstairs to join Mr. Pepper in the dining room, she walked along to Petteril's rooms. She went through the motion of knocking before she entered, even though she knew he wasn't home yet.

Stewart was pacing the sitting room floor, looking impatiently toward the door.

"Is his lordship back?" she asked brightly as he bowed.

"Not yet. Do you expect him to dine?"

"Who knows?" she said breezily. She didn't want him bolting straight to the inn as soon as she was safely out of the way in the dining room. She took a step nearer. "You just have to sit tight for a tiny bit longer. He knows who took the purse."

Stewart's hand jerked and was still.

"So why are you still being so silly about this?" she demanded. "He needs to know the full story before he can help you."

"I promised," he said.

She stared at him. "Then you value your promise to this thief?"

"Who am I to judge one moment of madness, when mine lasted two years?"

"So you should pay now when you are a good and respectable man?"

"That doesn't change what I did."

"Then why don't you go back to Scotland, confess your crimes and pay the price?"

He was silent.

"Because it isn't about you, is it?" she said. "It's all about the thief. The person Murray is blackmailing. Does Murray know who the thief is?"

Stewart shook his head. "Murray is the real villain in all of this. But he can't be arrested and tried without all the scandals coming out. There's only one way to silence a man like Murray."

Her eyes widened. "You'd murder him? And hang? Lord Petteril couldn't let that pass!"

"I know," Stewart said bleakly. "Hopefully, it won't come to that."

She tightened her lips. "You stay put, Mr. Stewart, or I'll have Benson tie you to a chair."

PIERS GAZED INTO THE empty eyes of the Scotsman who, to all intents and purposes, was a stranger to everyone.

"What makes you think I know this Murray?" the Scotsman sneered.

"Apart from the fact that his name caused you to sit down?" Piers said. "Probably that other fact, that you almost shot me to get at him. As it is, my hat will never recover."

"Prove it and I'll buy you another."

Piers sipped his brandy. "Actually, I probably could, but that is neither here nor there. Murray is no friend of mine."

"Nor of anyone else."

"Did he betray you?" Piers asked.

"No."

"Then I am guessing he betrayed your employer."

Something flickered in the distant eyes. Piers made the most of it.

"There are worse punishments than death," he remarked. "I believe we could help each other."

"I don't need help."

"I beg to differ. You have been here since Wednesday and were almost caught for shooting me instead of the right man. Murray is holed up in the Red Lion and likely to remain so until you get bored."

"He'll come out at night when he thinks I can't see him."

"He might," Piers said dubiously. "But there is a clearer solution. You go into the inn."

The Scotsman sneered some more. "Thanks for the advice. I prefer to have a way out."

"I could give you one." Beside Piers, Bill's elbow jerked and was still.

"Why would you do that?" the Scotsman asked.

"For a favour."

An odd relief showed in the Scotsman's face as he finished his ale. As though he finally understood Piers and was comfortable again. "Go on."

"Will Murray recognize you?" Piers asked.

The thin lips twisted. "Oh yes."

Piers smiled. "Then put the fear of God into him. Make him admit his crimes before witnesses. And then you can have him. For—er...Scottish justice."

The Scotsman considered, then pressed his lips together and nodded acknowledgement. "Question. Why don't *you* scare the wee rat into confession?"

"I'm not convinced he is scared enough of *me*."

The Scotsman did not buy that. His lips twisted. "Got something on you too, has he?"

"On a friend of mine."

The man's eyes were blank although the concept of a friend was alien. However, he did not appear to hold the weakness against Piers.

"Have it your way," he said, rising to his feet once more. "I'm sick of this place."

VERITY WIPED HER HANDS on her apron. They weren't dirty, but her palms were sweating and her stomach jumping with nerves as she walked into the kitchen.

It was a quiet evening, with only the regulars in the taproom. The inn's staying guests had eaten quietly either in the common room or in their own chambers. She had no money to give to Murray. And she had not yet stooped so low that she would give herself. There was only one solution. It would probably lose her this place and make next month even more difficult, but Hope and her family needed the money now.

Mrs. Barnes, an old friend of her mother's, sat at the kitchen table, yawning over a notebook of recipes. A cup of tea sat at her elbow.

"Ma'am? Can I have a word?"

"Is it still quiet in there?" Mrs. Barnes demanded.

Verity nodded. "I need to talk to you. Tell you something."

Mrs. Barnes looked at her quite closely. "Best have a cup of tea then," she said, nodding toward the chair next to her, while she filled another cup with weak tea. She reused the leaves after the guests got the best of them.

Verity sat, holding her trembling hands together in her lap and blurted out the tale of her child and her need to pay.

"It's the only way that works. If I stay at home with her, we starve. This way, she's got my sister, and I can pay her, make sure they can afford what they need, especially the doctor..."

Mrs. Barnes sighed, looking sorrowful. "I suppose I know why you didn't tell me at the outset."

"You wouldn't have taken me on, would you?"

"Probably not. I like the house to be respectable."

"Can I stay until I find somewhere else?"

"'Course you can, dear. It's not such an unusual story and I think no less of you for what happened. In fact, you might as well stay on—providing no one knows."

Verity swallowed, tears starting to her eyes. She hadn't expected such kindness. Should she tell the whole truth?

APRIL DID NOT LINGER over her dinner. Mr. Pepper was an amiable gentleman and kept up an impressive flow of small talk, but lawyers made her nervous. Besides, she couldn't tell whether or not he disapproved of her. She was restless, and he was clearly exhausted, for he asked permission to retire immediately after the meal.

Hiding her relief, April made sure he had everything he required, and left him to it.

After rejecting tea in the drawing room, she decided to go to the stables to pass the time with Benson and the horses. This would also serve the purpose of keeping her eyes open in case Stewart could not stop himself from going to the Red Lion.

She was almost too late. Wrapped in the old cloak she had hung near the side door of the house, she could hear furious whispers coming from the stables. Carter, the old head groom, and the other staff were enjoying a last mug of tea in the tack room, but Benson was absent, presumably because he was doing most of the whispering in the main stable.

She wasn't entirely surprised to see that the other whisperer was Stewart.

The voices turned off like a tap when they caught sight of her. After an instant, they remembered to bow.

"You weren't planning to go out, were you, Stewart?" she said pleasantly.

She was no longer the rescued street urchin, nor even their master's favoured maidservant. But still she cringed using this tone to her old friends.

Stewart met her gaze. "Yes, my lady."

"Even though his lordship forbade it?"

"His lordship doesn't know everything."

She took a step nearer. "Then he should! Tell *me*."

Stewart caught his breath. "On the way, then. One way or another I *have* to go!"

There was desperation in his voice. More, his intent was immovable.

"Why?" she demanded.

"Because you don't know what he'll do to her if she doesn't pay! Do I need to explain what he meant by accepting *payment in kind*?"

Her lips drew back in involuntary distaste. "No." She caught his arm as he brushed past her to the first stall, staying him until he looked at her. "From whom, Stewart?"

KATE CAMDEN WALKED in the gathering dusk, very aware of the man at her side. She wished she could take his arm, but he leaned too heavily on the stick.

"What is it?" he asked quietly.

"What is what?" she asked.

"Something troubles you. Something has always troubled you. Since I met you," he added deprecatingly, "what, four days ago?"

"Perhaps it is you."

"Is it?"

"No," she admitted. "I like you." With the admission, just how much she liked him washed over her in a wave. And yet, like every other liking, it was doomed. Only Darius had ever stood by her. No man would tolerate her story and marry her.

Marry her! No one married on such short acquaintance, not without a huge incentive.

So, now was the time to tell him, before she let him slip further into her heart; before he would feel too betrayed by the truth.

"I like you too," he said.

She smiled sadly. "No, you don't. You like what you think I am, what I have *let* you think I am."

His gaze remained steady on hers. "And what are you?"

She lifted her chin. "I am a fallen woman, wreathed in scandal and received nowhere. After all, I don't even have the wealth to make up for it to the most gazetted fortune hunters. I am dependent on my brother, who is kind and tolerant and frequently wishes me at the devil."

He was silent for several moments while she tried to form the protective ice around her heart.

"I don't believe that is true," he said.

She frowned in confusion. "What?"

"Sir Darius would miss you, should you ever leave him. What did you do to inspire this scandal?"

"I eloped with a man who abandoned me at the border."

"Bastard," said Captain Lyall. "Pardon my language. He was also an idiot."

"Thank you." She waited, but still he did not ask.

Instead, he said, "I have nothing either. A little prize money due to me, if they ever pay up. But there is hope. I shall think of something. In the meantime, may we not be friends?"

"F-friends?" she repeated.

He halted and turned to face her. His eyes were warm and unexpectedly humorous. "Friends who might develop an understanding. If I am less grumpy and find a way to make a living."

"But...but you have not even asked me if I *did*!"

"Did what?" he asked bending nearer.

"Gave myself to him! I did."

"I don't care," he said, and kissed her.

She could not help but kiss him back. He seemed to be very good at it.

When she could speak—and think—again, she demanded, "Why don't you care?"

He shrugged. "I'm not exactly pure either."

"But you're a man!"

"I'm glad you noticed. I've never really understood why that should make a difference. Did you love this bastard? I suppose you must have, or you wouldn't have meant to marry him."

"I *thought* I loved him. It was all I hung onto, through the scandal and the isolation. Now...I think I was in love with romance. Infatuation at best."

"Then there is hope you could love me? Damaged as I am."

Her fingers gripped the hair at his nape. "I might already. I don't recognize this feeling at all. But you have to understand, people still remember the scandal. It will count against you if you marry me."

"What people?"

She curled her lip. "Neil Murray, for one. I paid him to be silent because it's not fair on Darius to have it all raked up again. Now it's not fair on you either."

He drew back to peer into her face. "You *paid* him? The little worm...!"

"He wants more," she blurted. "But I can't ask Darius. He would know something was wrong and *annihilate* him."

"He'd need to fight me for the privilege," the captain said savagely. "Thank God I still have one strong arm!"

"Then he'll blab from spite—if he lives. And if he doesn't, you—or Darius—will hang for murder. There is a way out. He...he says he will settle for payment in kind."

Chapter Twelve

There was no time to change, or Stewart would merely have gone without her, so April arrived at the Red Lion in a crushed evening gown and old traveling cloak, but with an escort of two manservants.

There wasn't much conversation en route. Once, Stewart burst out, "He's been doing it for years, wherever he goes, in between other thefts and even during them. It's as if he can't help it. Everyone always pays, and he's never stopped."

Leaving a grim Benson to care for the horses, April said to Stewart. "Give me five minutes before you come in."

"You can't go in there alone!" Stewart objected. For the first time ever, he actually sounded shocked.

"Don't be silly. Mr. and Mrs. Barnes are always there. I don't want you murdering Murray before there's any need. Besides, if he bolts this way, you must catch him."

"Ap...my lady, the man's a rat! If he's cornered—"

April grinned. "Who'd feel cornered by me?" She sailed through the inn door, praying Stewart would obey her, for in reality, she was no one's lady.

At first glance, the common room looked empty. A hum of muffled voices, interspersed with occasional shouts of raucous laughter, drifted through the closed taproom door. And at the foot of the stairs, among the shadows, stood two figures, a man and a woman.

Neither of them appeared to notice her entrance, which suited April perfectly. She needed to learn.

She had spent much of her life trying not to be noticed, whether thieving or just avoiding trouble. She knew how to move silently—admittedly without skirts around her ankles, but still... She glided across the floor.

The couple in the shadows were oblivious. They stood so close together, they could have been lovers, only there was no love in the woman's stiff, trembling body. Only fear.

It was the maidservant, Verity. And looming over her was Murray.

It was Verity that Stewart cared for, Verity who was being blackmailed. But was she the one who stole the purse? Stewart had refused to tell her that. It would make sense if she was desperate to pay Murray off...

"I can't and I won't," the girl was saying. Although her voice trembled, she spoke with decision, as though she had rehearsed the words. "The money's already been sent to my family. I have nothing to give you."

"Not entirely true. I would have preferred the money, but you will have to do."

An abuser's deliberate, manipulative contempt. Time to intervene.

Then Verity took her by surprise. She lifted her head and April held her breath. Against the odds, the worm was turning, and April would not take that away from her.

"You're not listening, sir," Verity said. "You get nothing from me. Tell Mrs. Barnes if you like, but there's no point. She already knows. I told her this evening. No one else can hurt me."

Murray pushed himself closer to her, an ugly curl to his mouth although his voice remained soft. "Oh my dear, that is where you are wrong. *Everyone* can hurt you. Especially me." He grasped her arm. "Now, since you won't pay, you'll play. Upstairs."

Verity struggled instinctively, though clearly no match for Murray's strength.

Time for the viscountess.

"Unhand my maid, sir, this instant."

Both heads snapped round to stare at her. No wonder. She had spoken with such clear, icy sharpness she had startled herself.

She snapped her fingers and since Murray's grip had loosened in startlement, Verity stumbled toward her, gasping, "Lady Petteril!"

But Murray only smiled and bowed elaborately to her. "My dear lady, you have mistaken the girl. She's the tavern wench, not your ladyship's woman."

"On the contrary, the mistakes are all yours."

A flash of irritation crossed his face but he shrugged. "Have it your way, but the girl is a whore."

The front door swung open. *Stewart.* Damn. She needed another minute...

Malevolent triumph lit Murray's face. "She has a child out of wedlock," he said loudly, "and hides here to escape the shame. But if that is the character you want in your servants..."

April swung around in a last desperate attempt to prevent Stewart from committing murder, but the case was worse than that. It wasn't only one footfall she had heard. Miss Camden and Captain Lyall had entered and heard everything. They halted, the captain frowning with distaste, the lady's eyes flashing with anger.

Stewart brushed past them with purpose. Behind his grimness was an odd sort of anticipation that was almost pleasure. *This* was the man who had charged so happily into the fight at the Queen's Head to save Lord Petteril...

"Didn't know that, did you, Stewart?" Murray jeered.

Kate Camden's hand shot out and caught Stewart's arm. He swung around to face her, dislodging her arm, and for an instant, they stared at each other. Something passed between them, some understanding that turned April's certainty into confusion.

Stewart *did* know Kate. Had she taken the purse after all and let Stewart bury it for her? Had it been her at the folly? Was she yet another victim of Murray's blackmail?

April wondered how he had lived this long.

"What the devil's going on?" a man demanded, thumping down the stairs. Sir Darius Camden, fully dressed, though his hair stood on end and his cravat was askew. "What are you doing down here in the middle of the night, Kate?"

"It's not yet ten of the clock," Kate replied mildly. "What are *you* doing down here? I thought you were having an early night?"

"Been in bed so long I can't sleep," Sir Darius complained, crossing the room toward his sister. "Thought I'd have a brandy before Barnes retires."

"Excellent idea," April said. She caught and held Stewart's gaze. "Perhaps you'd bring a bottle from the taproom while we sit down."

Stewart opened his mouth to refuse.

"I'll fetch it," Verity muttered and bolted through the taproom door. Stewart transferred his glare to Murray, who smirked, clearly under the illusion that the valet would never strike him in the presence of his master's lady. Not least because Murray knew the secret of his past.

"Shall we sit down?" April said. "I think it's time to end this mystery."

"Very kind of you ma'am," Darius said stiffly. "But I don't believe we're acquainted."

"This is Lady Petteril, Darius," Kate said. "My lady, I'm sure you have already guessed that this is my brother, Sir Darius Camden."

"Oh!" Sir Darius peered closer, then bowed. "Saw you from my window, now you mention it. Your ladyship's servant."

"Sir Darius," April returned civilly. "Gentlemen, do sit down. I'm afraid Mr. Murray will be joining us because secrecy will no longer serve anyone."

Murray, still imagining he held the whip hand, took the seat next to the door. Captain Lyall eyed him with distaste. Sir Darius sat on his sister's other side.

April took the seat at the head of table, pretending to be in control. In reality, her blood seemed to be humming with excitement, spurring her on as she imagined Petteril's surprise, Petteril's pride in her, when she solved the mystery.

"Forgive me, Miss Camden," she said, "but when did Mr. Murray first ask you for money?"

Colour swept up into Kate's face. Lyall's breath caught. Sir Darius gazed at his sister, his heavy jaw dropping.

Kate lifted her chin. "On Wednesday afternoon, almost as soon as we arrived. I believe he overheard our names when we introduced ourselves to the innkeeper."

"The fellow asked you for money?" Sir Darius demanded, his voice rising with incipient fury.

April had her answer, and yet it felt wrong. She had never truly imagined that Kate would steal from her brother, and let a man be arrested in her place, to placate a blackmailer. She had never seemed that kind of...helpless. April had really only asked to eliminate her, and yet Kate would have had access to her brother's room when he was in it. Easy enough to pick up the purse unseen...

Stewart must have caught her with it and, because he knew Murray's little ways, helped her by hiding the purse.

Only, all the money had still been in the purse when Petteril found it. Perhaps he had simply advised Kate not to pay and buried the purse until it was all over.

Movement at the taproom door distracted her. Verity stumbled through, bearing a tray with two bottles and several of the inn's better glasses.

At once, Stewart went to her, closed the door, and took the tray from her. She cast him a quick, soft smile.

No, April thought in frustration. Stewart might have helped Miss Camden, but his feelings were all for Verity.

Then the front door opened in a draught of cold air and darkness and Lord Petteril walked in with a complete stranger.

He looked windswept and tired and yet impossibly elegant. And suddenly, April cared nothing for solving the mystery first. She was just so pleased to see him that she jumped to her feet, grinning.

Murray sprang up at the same time, and launched himself not at the newcomers, or even the door, but straight at April.

He cannoned into her, knocking the breath from her body, spinning her around, one arm clamping her to his body. Something pricked at her throat. She knew cold steel well enough to recognize a blade. She froze.

Yet her brain still seemed to work. The stranger with Petteril held a wicked, double-barrelled pistol pointed straight at her. No, not at her, at Murray, cowering behind her, using her as a shield.

Petteril had found the shooter.

The shooter who had already proved he didn't care who he hurt in the process of killing his man.

There was an almighty crash as Stewart dropped the tray, but the gunman's hand never wavered.

Oh, no, I won't be dead already! I won't. Piers…

PIERS HAD MADE A TERRIBLE mistake.

A series of mistakes.

He had assumed he could control the assassin.

The pistol was hardly unexpected, but stupidly, Piers had never even thought of a rare, double-barrelled one. The Scot could shoot twice.

And even more stupidly, he had never imagined that April would be here, sitting cosily around a table with Neil Murray.

Desperately, futilely, he launched himself in front of the assassin, just as he squeezed the trigger and the world exploded in noise.

Through it, Piers recognized the weird similarity to the Queen's Head, when he had tried to prevent a different shot, but this, *this* catastrophe was blinding, so terrible that the blackness surged into his head, even as he crashed into the assassin, who staggered under his weight.

And then something wonderful happened. The blade clattered to the floor and Murray bent over, clutching his chest and wheezing and April ran to Piers.

At last, he registered what he had seen. Risking the knife, April had elbowed Murray hard in the chest and slid free. Probably at the same time as the shot was fired, though where the ball had gone was anyone's guess because it wasn't in him.

And then nothing else mattered because she was alive, landing like a whirlwind in his arms.

He retained enough sense to snap, "Justice," at the assassin striding past them to Murray, and then he gave in to the clamouring of his heart and kissed his wife, releasing all the passion, all the relief and fear, wonder, and joy that had been building in him for months. On and on, he kissed her, while she clung to him as if to her only lifeline.

The world came back very slowly.

"What the devil happened in here?" That sounded like Barnes, bolting from the taproom, no doubt with assorted drinkers in tow.

"I say," said Sir Darius in affronted tones, and April began to giggle.

The sound was like music to Petteril's ears. He drew back, though he kept his arm around her waist. Heat burned his cheeks, but he refused to acknowledge it.

A quick glance showed him that the assassin had Murray by the collar. The captive was almost gibbering with fear.

"Is he the thief?" Barnes demanded. "Did he take Sir Darius's purse?"

"Alas not," Piers said. "But he is wanted up in Scotland for murder and robbery."

"I heard a gunshot," Barnes insisted. "And why's this glass all over the floor? Don't just stand there, Verity, clear it up! And light some candles for our guests!"

While Verity rushed off to obey, Piers raised his quizzing glass to his eye and scanned the room. Even in the dim light, he could make out the hole in the large, wooden mantelpiece.

"You really are a shockingly bad shot," he said to the assassin.

"I was giving your girl a chance to get out the way," the Scotsman said, not very convincingly. "Besides, I don't need to be a good shot with the gun right at his head."

He demonstrated, resting the pistol barrel against Murray's temple.

Kate squeaked with horror and Murray squeezed his eyes shut.

"Best take him to Edinburgh," Piers said hastily. "If he confessed to the robbery and the murder."

"Oh, he did. We all heard, except you." The assassin grinned with alarming ferocity, but at least he lowered the gun, even pocketed it before shoving his captive toward the door.

"My lord! My lady!" Murray cried. "Don't let him take me! I only said what he wanted me to because otherwise he'd kill me. He'll *kill* me, my lady! Oh, have pity!"

"You recognize him, then?" Piers asked Murray interestedly. "Who is he?"

Murray stared from him to the Barneses, to the Camdens and the captain, and to Stewart. And must have realized that not only had he run out of friends but to reveal how he knew the assassin would remove any last remnant of pity for a respectable man.

He tried another tack. "You wrong me! I am a good man! I—"

"Stow it," growled the Viscountess Petteril.

Piers's lips twitched. The assassin winked at her and dragged his captive away out the door. Everyone watched them go, with varying expressions of bafflement, anger, relief, and doubt. Apart from Verity, who concentrated on sweeping up the mess of glass on the floor, and Stewart, who smiled quietly before turning and taking the broom and pan from Verity. He swept up while she took the mop from the bucket to wash the brandy-spattered floor, and everyone else turned to gaze at Piers and April.

"What just happened?" Kate enquired.

"Do I need to hear this?" Mr. Barnes asked.

"No," said Piers.

Barnes stamped back off to the taproom and his wife, after opening and closing her mouth once, waddled off to the kitchen.

Piers ushered his lady to a seat at the table. This time, he sat on the end, hemming her in.

As Captain Lyall and the Camdens sat back down, April spoke to Stewart. "You and Verity had better join us."

Stewart glanced over and hesitated. His eyes flickered to Piers, and he nodded curtly, before marching toward the kitchen, dustpan in one hand, Verity's bucket in the other. "One moment."

"What's to do, my lord?" Camden asked. "Is this about my purse? Do you know who took it?"

"Yes." Piers delved into his pocket and laid the leather purse on the table.

Camden uttered an exclamation and snatched it up, pulling the strings apart and rummaging inside with one finger. "Good Lord. Is it all still there?"

"So far as I can judge," Piers replied.

"Where in the world did you find it?"

"Buried," Piers replied, very aware of his wife sitting so close to him, touching at shoulder and arm and thigh. She could have shifted further away but she didn't. Stewart and Verity hurried toward them, Stewart scowling and carrying a fresh bottle and some more glasses on a tray. Verity looked nervous.

Stewart held a chair for her, and she seemed to collapse into it from sheer surprise. Hooking another with his foot, Stewart dragged it over and sat beside her before pouring brandy into several glasses and pushing them in front of each of the motley group, including Verity and himself.

Watching, Captain Lyall's lips quirked upward. He reached for his glass.

"For the shock," Piers explained. He curled his fingers around the stem of the glass. "The purse is with its owner so we could say there is no crime. If we go through the magistrate and make formal accusations, untold innocent lives will suffer when, to some degree, we are all to blame."

"Don't see how you work that out," Darius said dubiously.

"I believe it would have been returned to you the very day you noticed it was missing," Piers said. "If only Stewart, my valet, had not been arrested."

He held Stewart's gaze and the valet nodded curtly.

"The devil," Camden said. "Then he did take it after all?"

"No," Piers said, and made his decision. He didn't know any of them well, but he thought he had their measure. Besides, he really had no choice now. "I propose to lay the whole story before you, and then we must agree on the best way forward. You, Sir Darius, as the victim, must have the largest say."

"Very well," Camden said testily, "but who took the wretched thing in the first place? And how do you know? Did they confess?"

"No," Piers admitted. "But it all comes down to opportunity. Sir Darius locked his door when he went to the taproom that night."

"I did," Camden agreed, looking pleased. "Ha," he added to his sister.

"How do you know it was locked?" April demanded.

"Because I'm fairly sure that Stewart tried the door. He only buried the purse because he couldn't get into Sir Darius's room to leave it there."

Stewart's smile was twisted. By way of admission, he raised his glass to Piers.

"He tried the door while I was in the taproom?" Camden asked, to be sure he understood.

"Yes. He went upstairs with Murray, where he indeed only stayed a minute. Outside, I expect he came across the thief trying to get into your chamber."

"How could the thief have taken it if the door was locked?" Kate demanded.

Piers did not look at April who was quite an efficient picker of locks. "Because the thief did not take it from his chamber. She took it from the taproom."

"Eh?" said Camden.

"She?" Captain Lyall repeated, startled.

"As I say, it comes down to opportunity," Piers said evenly. "The opportunity arose when you, Sir Darius, absently picked up your purse before going down to the taproom. I expect you took it out in an equally absent manner and our thief took the chance."

"I did," Stewart said.

Camden glared at him. "*Will* you make up your mind? Did you or did you not steal my purse?"

"He didn't," Verity said fiercely. "I told everyone he didn't at the time. *I* took it."

"Verity," Stewart warned.

But she was looking directly at Camden. "I'm sorry. I don't know what came over me. I've never stolen anything in my life before. But you were pulling things frantically out of your pocket, looking for your handkerchief before you sneezed, and I just saw it there on the bench beside you. I got no excuse, sir, except I was weary and just for an instant it seemed to solve everything for me while you wouldn't miss a few coins. While you were sneezing and blowing your nose, I picked it up and dropped it in my apron pocket."

"Aprons," April repeated, staring at Piers. "So that's why you looked so struck about them!"

"I saw suddenly how it could have been done," Piers admitted. "And it made sense. Only Verity was in and out of the taproom all night, and we knew Stewart was protecting a woman. Miss Camden—forgive me, ma'am—was a possibility, and could have taken it at some other time, but she would have had no need to give the purse to Stewart, either to hide it or to give it back."

"I'm so sorry, sir," Verity said, wiping the tears streaming down her face. "I was at my wits' end."

"Why?" asked Lyall. "Was that blackguard Murray blackmailing you, too?"

"Not then," Verity whispered. "My—"

"One of her family was taken ill," Stewart said. "They couldn't afford both the doctor and food, so Verity was frantic with worry and not thinking straight."

"As soon as I'd done it, I was ashamed of myself," Verity said, crying harder. Stewart pushed a large, white handkerchief into her hand and she wiped at her eyes. "I thought of taking it right back to you, sir, saying I found it on the floor, but then I thought I couldn't lie to your face, so I thought I'd leave it in your room for you to find. So I crept upstairs as soon as I had a moment and was just trying your door when Mr. Stewart came out of Mr. Murray's room and saw me."

She sniffed and blew her nose. "He asked what I was up to going into a gentleman's room at that time of night, and I just blurted out what I'd done. Most'd think I was trying to steal something else from the gentleman, but Mr. Stewart believed me."

"I've met a few thieves in my time," Stewart said gruffly, "and you aren't one." He transferred his gaze to Piers. "I told her to keep watch while I tried the door—and found it was locked. So we decided I should take the purse with me. If Sir Darius discovered it was gone, the inn would have been torn apart and Verity found out. We decided to return it in the morning instead, when Verity would have the keys from Mrs. Barnes to clean the rooms. So I took it away with me and buried it at the folly."

"Only you never had time," April said, "because Mr. Lindon came and arrested you."

"It's a judgement on us," Verity whispered. "Because of what I did, and because Mr. Stewart tried to help me. I should never have let him. I should never have touched the purse in the first place. I can't believe I did..."

"We all have bad moments," Kate Camden said unexpectedly. "Moments of badness, or just utter foolishness that bear untold consequences for the rest of our lives." She fixed Piers suddenly with her bright gaze. "That's what you meant, isn't it? That we are all responsible for the way the world judges women and servants, and those of lesser degree. They tried to give it back, and I for one, would be happy to say no more about it."

Sir Darius frowned. "You would?"

Kate met her brother's gaze. "There but for the grace of God, Darius..."

Camden sighed. "Then I suppose I'd better be the silly fool who left the purse in the carriage and made a fuss for nothing. I'd better go out and find the dashed thing."

"I'll come with you," Lyall said, hauling himself to his feet. "I could be interested in buying one. One day. If you'd kindly show me what to look for."

"And after *that*," Darius said, scowling at Piers. "I want to know what was going on with that Murray fellow."

Piers smiled amiably and rose as soon as the door closed behind them. "Time to go home, I think. Some mysteries are better left just as they are."

Chapter Thirteen

April rode home beside her husband by the light of the moon and a lantern borrowed from the Red Lion. Stewart and Benson rode behind at a respectful distance.

"I hesitate to ask," Petteril had said to Benson as he mounted the weary Professor, "but what did you see of the man I arrived with?"

"I saw him leave again on his own horse. After he'd tied a whining man to another, which he led away. As you ordered, I didn't intervene. Is he the law, your man?"

"I have hopes," Lord Petteril said, somewhat ruefully. "Foolishly optimistic, I daresay."

"Who *is* that other Scotsman?" April asked as their horses trotted along the bridle path. "Because if he's the law, I'm—"

"He's a paid killer. Murray recently committed a robbery in Edinburgh, in which he killed a man and bolted with the proceeds, leaving his accomplices to take the blame. Someone hanged for it, I believe. But one of the accomplices felt strongly enough to send our man to exact vengeance."

"He had that look about him," April said without much surprise. More than the look. He would have shot her without a second thought, just to get Murray. Just as he had almost killed Petteril.

Lord Petteril shivered. But April could only feel warmth and wonder because she had survived, and because when she had fled to his arms, he had held her and kissed her *like that...*

Did he regret it? Would he see her now as his wife?

Petteril said, "We had a chat about justice. Brandy Bill's contribution to the conversation was invaluable. But whether he really will take Murray to the sheriff in Edinburgh is anyone's guess. He did seem to like the idea of official retribution, but..."

"On the road, he will probably revert to type. Murray might blackmail him out of it."

Petteril snorted.

"You meant it to happen," she pointed out. "You brought him there."

Petteril's lips compressed. "At first, I thought I could just use our assassin to scare Murray into a confession. But if we'd taken him to the magistrate and charged him with extortion, he would have ruined Stewart, Verity, Kate Camden and who knows who else on the way. Somehow, he'd have found out about the Lindons' mess and used that to escape. I couldn't let him go on. It is a particularly *nasty* crime, blackmail. Ruining lives whether his victims pay or not, driving people..."

He broke off.

"I know," she said quickly. She smiled encouragingly. "Maybe you've turned a soulless killer into a useful member of society as a hunter of fugitives."

"Hmm," Petteril said dubiously.

"Either way, it *is* justice," April said firmly. "And Murray doesn't care. A shot to the head is quicker than the noose." She lowered her voice, aware of Stewart and Benson some distance behind, because words could carry on the breeze. "There's one thing I don't understand: what is between Stewart and Kate?"

His eyebrows flew up. "Nothing that I know of."

"She's too aware of him. And there was a look when they met this evening."

"Then I expect Stewart recognizes a victim of Murray's blackmail when he sees one."

"That makes sense," she allowed, thinking it over. He might even have offered help obliquely. It would be like him. She drew in her breath. "Um, I have a confession to make too."

The lantern light played over the deep frown on his brow. "Go on."

"I sort of offered Verity a position."

His shoulders eased. "You may employ whoever you wish in the house."

"Really? Mrs. Hicks keeps reminding me I don't have a personal maid and it was all I could think of to make Murray release her before Stewart stormed in." She took a deep breath. "Besides, it isn't right that she has to live apart from her child. She could bring it here."

Petteril was silent.

"We don't have to," she said anxiously. "I know she isn't considered respectable, but we could call her a widow."

"It's a kind idea, and I suspect you are matchmaking. Perhaps you should consult Stewart first. And consider all the ramifications. Is Mrs. Barnes throwing her out?"

"Not unless the baby becomes public knowledge. Kate and the captain know, but they won't tell—Kate has suffered enough from gossip herself."

He nodded, but she had the feeling his attention had moved on. She didn't mind. He was leaving the matter to her, trusting her, even though as the viscountess, she was blundering in the dark.

Tomorrow, she had to take tea with the Lindons, face the denizens of a world who would despise her for her birth and pity Petteril for having married her. Could she carry that off with any conviction?

He had kissed her as though he meant it. Perhaps she could do anything after all.

Perhaps...

Haybury Court rose above the trees, a few scattered lights still showing. When she had first come here in the spring, she had been awed because it looked like a castle, like a prettier Tower of London. And she got to live in it. Now she was its mistress.

It had never really been his lordship's home. And it had certainly never been the home he wanted. But she could make it so...

Perhaps.

Her heart began to beat faster. Change was in the air again. She might have been afraid but for once, she embraced it.

Jem, the once insolent stable lad who had now adopted Benson as his mentor, had waited up to help Benson care for the horses.

Stewart entered the house with Petteril and April by the side door, which he locked behind him.

"Go to bed, Stewart," Petteril said. "I think we all need a good sleep."

"Very good, my lord." Stewart inclined his head, once more the respectful gentleman's gentleman. He hesitated, then. "Thank you for what you said and did. It means a lot and I won't forget."

Most people would, then, have pointed out that the matter would have been more easily settled if Stewart had explained things in the first place. Lord Petteril didn't.

"I expect I'm counting on it," he said vaguely. "Good night, Stewart."

"Good night, sir. My lady." He bowed and strode away toward the servants' stairs at the back of the house.

As they reached the main hall, Barclay emerged. "May I lock the front door, my lord?"

"If you please. Good night, Barclay."

Petteril lit another candle from the one burning at the foot of the stairs and gave it to April. They walked up the stairs in silence. Had she ever been so aware of him? So aware of her own failings? She could not even make her throat work properly to invite him to her sitting room.

"Are you tired?" he asked abruptly.

"Not really. I suppose you must be, having ridden so far."

"My brain seems too busy to be tired. Care for a nightcap?"

She smiled with relief. "Yes, please. I seem to be developing a taste for good brandy."

"There's the port we brought back from the Peninsula—I'll bring that, too."

He opened her door for her, then strode off along the passage. April entered, trying to distract herself with lighting the lamps and candles.

Yesterday, Lord Petteril could have died. Tonight, *she* almost did. And he would never have known what was in her heart. Things needed to be said. She wished she could express herself better. Like Petteril did, when he bothered. She liked the way he spoke, the words he used, so light and humorous... and occasionally devastating. But always apt.

Only when she heard him come back, glass clanking faintly against glass, did she panic because she hadn't even glanced in the mirror. She probably looked like a street urchin again, rather than Lady Petteril. But he had always known what she was...

She sat on the chaise longue, where there was room for him to sit beside her if he chose. Her heart drumming, she asked for port and still wondered at the novelty of *him* serving *her*.

He placed her glass on the low table in front of her, where she could easily reach it, and moved to the chair opposite. At least he drew it nearer to her.

If she sat at his feet, would he stroke her hair again? Could she say the words then?

He stretched out his long legs, relaxing into the chair with his head back, his glass held lightly in his elegant, aristocratic hand.

He is comfortable with me, she thought in wonder. And somehow, that silent comfort spread, and she sipped her port, letting all the memories of Portugal and Spain drift through her mind. Getting to know him in the sunshine, becoming his equal.

What she had with him was good. Too good to risk.

He straightened his head and raised the glass to his lips.

Life is short.

"Is it time?" she blurted.

He blinked. "Time?"

She took another sip for courage. "I want you to know something. I love you."

She heard his breath catch but could not look at him. "I don't need a response to that. I just want you to know. It's not awe, or gratitude or some fairytale infatuation. I always loved you. Even when I was a boy. Now I'm your wife and I love you more."

His eloquent lordship was silent for so long she wanted to weep, because she had misjudged. She'd got it wrong.

He leaned forward and set down his glass. "I saw you, once. In the town house attic, just after I'd told you you had to become a girl again."

She blinked at him, uncomprehending. Was he changing the subject?

"I went up to see what you had found that might be of any use to you, and I saw you dancing in a shaft of dusty sunlight. Delighting in the unexpected, in a ridiculous old gown that almost drowned you. I had never seen anything, anyone so beautiful."

She stopped breathing. "I didn't know you were there," she managed at last, shakily.

"I went away very quickly. Hid, I suppose. I do a lot of hiding, as you know."

She swallowed convulsively. "I'm glad you thought I was beautiful. I wish I really was. For you."

He rose and her heart skittered as he came and sat beside her. "April, you *are* beautiful, and not just to me. But that's not what I meant. I knew when I saw you in the attic. That I love you."

He took her hand from her lap and held it, his grip gentle yet warm and strong. It all added to the sheer wonder of his words.

She clung to his fingers, staring at him. "You l-love me? Me?"

His lips quirked in the way she cherished, the smile lighting his eyes. "You."

"But you never..." She broke off, heat burning up into her face.

"I know something of your past. I would never force myself on you. What kind of love would that be?"

Force? "I am your wife."

She stared up at him, desperately trying to read his eyes—impossible when he chose to hide. But she heard the rapidity of his breathing, and in a sudden movement, she raised their joined hands to his chest. His heart beat strongly against her fingers.

"I'm not afraid," she whispered. "Not of you."

The veil lifted from his eyes, whether by accident or design, and she gasped, just as he lowered his head.

This was not the wild, hard kiss that had overwhelmed her at the inn. This was so gentle that she ached. And yet it melted her from the inside out.

He rose, drawing her to her feet and into his arms. "Then it *is* time?" he asked, just a little huskily.

She smiled. "It is."

She threaded her fingers through his, wondering which of them was shaking, and led him across the room to her bedchamber. After that, he did the leading; and with patience, tenderness, and ultimately passion, taught her astounding new joy.

Now, there was no going back. Ever. And that was best of all.

Watch out for *Petteril's Christmas*, coming autumn 2024!

About the Author

MARY LANCASTER IS A USA Today bestselling author of award winning historical romance and historical fiction. She lives in Scotland with her husband, one of three grown-up kids, and a small dog with a big personality.

Her first literary love was historical fiction, a genre which she relishes mixing up with romance and adventure in her own writing. Several of her novels feature actual historical characters as diverse as Hungarian revolutionaries, medieval English outlaws, and a family of eternally rebellious royal Scots. To say nothing of Vlad the Impaler.

More recently, she has enjoyed writing light, fun Regency romances, with occasional forays into the Victorian era. With its slight change of emphasis, *Petteril's Thief*, was her first Regency-set historical mystery.

CONNECT WITH MARY ON-line – she loves to hear from readers:

Email Mary: Mary@MaryLancaster.com

Website: http://www.MaryLancaster.com

Newsletter sign-up: https://marylancaster.com/newsletter/

Facebook: https://www.facebook.com/mary.lancaster.1656

Facebook Author Page: https://www.facebook.com/MaryLancasterNovelist/

Twitter: @MaryLancNovels https://twitter.com/MaryLancNovels

Bookbub: https://www.bookbub.com/profile/mary-lancaster

Printed in Great Britain
by Amazon

44795872R00091